12

Melissa Hosack

WP

Whimsical Publications, LLC

Florida

To purchase the authorized electronic edition of *12*, visit
www.whimsicalpublications.com

Cover art by Janet Durbin
Editing by Brieanna Robertson

Published in the United States by
Whimsical Publications, LLC
Florida

ISBN-13: 978-1-936167-79-1

Printed in the United States of America

The ground shook again, and the screams grew louder.

The ground shook again, and the screams grew louder.

Scott whipped around, aiming the camera behind them where most of the shouts had come from. He walked backwards down the sidewalk, yet he picked up speed as he moved. "We need to go faster," he said with urgency in his tone.

Nikki spun to see what had him so concerned just as the ground shook again. She twisted her ankle and nearly fell, but managed to see enough to terrify her as she righted herself.

When the ground trembled, it shook nearby buildings enough that large pieces of concrete were falling from the sky. Chunks of the buildings were cracking off from over thirty stories up, falling to the earth with enough force to smash the roof of a car. Glass shattered in the windows of the buildings from the force of the quaking ground.

The sidewalk under her feet shook again and was followed by pebbles raining down around them from the building that rose above their heads.

"Get into the street!" Scott hollered. "Get away from the building!" He gave Nikki a less than gentle shove, causing her to stumble forward.

Tony and Pearson, who had been looking out into the chaos the streets had become with its speeding vehicles and frantic people darting in between, turned to see what the commotion was all about.

Upon seeing the falling brick and concrete smashing into the pavement, Tony raced into the street. His eyes were completely on the buildings instead of the traffic he'd just plunged into.

"Tony, look out!" Nikki cried, cringing as a car swerved around him, missing by inches.

He spun around in surprise to face an oncoming motorcycle.

The man on the motorcycle waved a hand frantically at Tony. He screamed something in Japanese as he motioned Tony to move out of his way. Though there was plenty of time for the man to stop, he didn't even slow down. He continued yelling in Japanese, his arm waving in the air.

His eyes widening, Tony stumbled backwards, trying to get out of the way. He didn't get completely clear, and when the motorcycle zoomed past, it ran over his foot.

Tony gave a holler of pain and nearly collapsed to the ground. He lifted his left foot and clutched it between his hands. "Asshole," he seethed through clenched teeth. Wanting to test the amount of damage that had been done, he gingerly lowered his foot to the ground. This was followed by another growl of agony. "I think it's broken."

Scott cursed under his breath, shooting the retreating motorcycle a glare. To Tony, he said, "We'll help you. Don't worry about it." Over his shoulder, he called, "Pearson, give me a hand!" Moving quickly, he hefted one of Tony's arms over his shoulder, keeping the video camera in his free hand. After a moment of no assistance, he said shortly, "Pearson! I said give me a hand!" When he received no response, he turned toward the younger man with a look of impatience.

Pearson was still standing on the sidewalk, frozen in terror. He watched as the buildings on the next street crumbled apart.

"Pearson!" Scott shouted in warning as the ground gave another violent shake. "Pearson, get off the sidewalk!"

Pearson glanced up at Scott with wide eyes as if finally hearing him, but the warning came too late. He was standing too close to the buildings.

As his friends watched in horror, a chunk of concrete the size of an end table broke away from one of the upper floors of a nearby building. In the mere moments it took to fall, it picked up speed. The concrete came down on Pearson's head with a sickening crack. It crushed him underneath it, snapping bones like twigs. They saw blood gush a second before the stone hit the pavement. Then it connected with sidewalk, sending chips of concrete and dust into the air.

Nikki screamed. She screamed and screamed and screamed until she thought her lungs might burst. While Scott and Tony coughed from the dust and rubble in the air, still she screamed. And when the dust finally cleared, making it easy to see the ruined, bloodied remains of their friend, she broke down into heaving sobs.

ACKNOWLEDGEMENTS

I would like to dedicate this book to my wonderful husband Jeremy who did more research than I could have ever expected to make this book happen. This was his idea, and he definitely helped me put in the work for it. Without him, the details about certain prophesied events may have been missed. So thank you!

CHAPTER 1

Pyramid of Khufu
Giza, Egypt
Just Outside Cairo
December 20th, 2012
Lilly Singh

Lilly Singh stooped down outside the infamous Khufu pyramid and ran her hand along the wall of the ancient structure, her expression one of awe. She couldn't believe she was actually here, actually getting to see the pyramids she'd fallen in love with when she was a little girl.

Her friends back home in North Carolina thought she was crazy for majoring in archaeology, but it was her biggest passion. While they were out spending money on booze and designer footwear, she'd been saving up for this trip, the trip of a lifetime. A smile spread across her lips as she realized that sacrificing her social life had been more than worth it.

She slid her fingertips along the wall, marveling at the design, at the effort that must have gone into making such a magnificent piece of history. She leaned in closer to get a better look at the stone when a shadow fell over the pyramid wall.

"You're American," a voice commented, sounding surprised.

Lilly paused a beat, wondering if she could simply ignore the person. Deciding that wasn't the most polite option, she stood and slowly turned to face the owner of the voice. She had to tilt her head back to look up into the face of the man towering over her.

He was tall, at least six feet. He had sun-bleached blond hair peeking out from underneath a large, ridiculous-looking cowboy hat. He was muscled in all the right places, and there was an adorable dimple in his left cheek. She placed him at around her age, perhaps a year or two older. She guessed him to be about twenty-two.

She couldn't hold back her sigh of agitation or keep her arms from crossing over her chest in a blatant show of impatience. "What makes you say that?" she asked, her tone lacking any real interest to hear his explanation. Her appearance didn't give away her place of residence. Her family was of Indian decent. Her parents had moved to America when she was three. With her dark skin and jet-black hair, she looked more Middle Eastern than American.

The blond cowboy smiled. "University of North Carolina," he said, tapping the student ID attached to her shirt. He motioned to an identical badge attached to his own collar. "Haven't seen you around campus before, but we run into each other in Egypt. Weird."

She'd completely forgotten about her student ID. Many places gave discounted tours if a trip was school related, so she constantly kept it nearby. Seeing as archaeology was her major and the University had helped her make arrangements, she loosely considered this to be a school related trip. Unfortunately, it made her prey to homesick, college-aged Americans.

She eyed the cowboy for a moment, deciding on the best way to get rid of him. She'd spent the past two years avoiding people of the opposite sex because she didn't want a relationship to interfere with her trip. She sure as hell wasn't about to have a fling while she was here. Steeling him with a hard look, she said, "You mean you're suddenly talking to me because, for once, it's your looks that stand out in a crowd? You want to use me to blend in better."

Instead of being offended, he smiled. "Nah, I don't mind. I travel a lot. I'm used to being the palest face in the room."

Lilly wouldn't call him pale. His skin was a nice bronzed color, causing the bright blue of his eyes to stand out. She could tell his skin was tanned from outdoor activities, not a product of a tanning bed or simply good genetics. He was obviously a very active individual and a traveler to boot. She hated to admit that he was actually somewhat interesting.

That thought made her shift her weight in annoyance. She really had to get rid of him. Her original plan to get him to leave hadn't worked. That meant she would have to try a new, though equally rude, angle. "I don't date cowboys, Tex."

"Tex?" he asked with a chuckle.

"Tex," she repeated. "Like Texas, where all you cowboys

are from."

This time, he burst out into laughter. "I don't consider myself a cowboy, far from it. And my family is from Jersey."

"Well, I don't date...Jersians."

"Jersians?" he asked on a laugh. Hooking his thumbs into the front pockets of his jeans, he squinted at her through the bright sunlight. "Before you give me the full list of people you don't date, how about we introduce ourselves?" His grin widened as he offered a hand for her to shake. "I'm Christian, and I don't date blondes."

She reluctantly took his hand. "Lilly. And I don't date Christians."

His fingers tightened over hers in a friendly, amused manner. "Do you mean the religious type or those with the name Christian?"

"Both," she assured. "Do you think my Muslim parents would approve? The name alone is enough to freak them out."

Christian released her hand and his thumb returned to his pocket. "Good thing I'm not looking for a date then." He took a step back to give her some space. "I just figured being in a place full of unfamiliar people, it might be nice to sit down to dinner with someone remotely familiar. It beats eating alone."

"You're no more familiar to me than anyone else here."

"I'd bet if I say the name Professor Dayton to anyone else in Egypt, they'd have no clue who I was talking about."

Though she tried to hide it, she knew he saw her smirk at the mention of the wacky professor.

Pretending as if he hadn't seen her grin, he said, "Whatever you prefer, though. It was just a thought." He slipped his backpack off and began riffling around inside. Pulling out a notebook, he scribbled something on a piece of paper and tore it free. He handed her the slip of paper with an easy smile. "In case you're bored one night and change your mind, here's the number to my cell."

Lilly hesitantly took the paper from him. "I won't change my mind," she warned.

Christian gave a careless shrug. "Then perhaps we'll run into each other on campus some time." He gave her a casual wave over his shoulder as he loped off toward the entrance of the pyramid.

Lilly watched him jog away, relief flooding through her

with every inch that grew between them. "Sorry, Tex," she said under her breath, though he was too far away to be able to hear her. "This trip is too important to let anything get in the way."

Nagoya, Japan
Erika Kimura

Erika stared at her fiancé Tye Yoshida and fought the urge to stomp her foot. "This is important to me," she said tensely, trying to keep her hands from balling into angry fists.

"Yes, but this meeting is important to me," he reminded her. "Erika, this is a big opportunity for us. I make this deal and we'll have the money for that fancy apartment you've had your eye on." He wrapped his arms around her waist and pulled her toward him. "I know how badly you'd like a nicer place. Wouldn't it be nice to live somewhere that the hot water works consistently?"

She sighed and pushed him away from her. "I want you to stay alive more than I want some flashy apartment."

Running his hands through his thick black hair, Tye made a sound of frustration. "The world is not going to end tomorrow," he said a little harshly. "If I cancel this meeting to follow you to America, do you know how that's going to look?"

"Like you don't want to die?"

"No," he argued, "like I panic without cause. I promise you, if Japan starts to sink, I'll hop a charter to China."

"It will be too late then," she snapped, snatching her duffel bag out of the back of their taxi. She counted to ten, trying to calm herself. As she slung the bag over her shoulder and turned to face him, her expression was pleading. "I'm begging you. Come with me, Tye. Please."

He glanced over his shoulder at the closest entrance to the airport. "I don't have anything with me. No clothes, no toiletries."

"We'll buy you more!" she pleaded.

"Cancel my business meeting *and* buy a new wardrobe? We definitely can't afford that." He stared at his feet for a moment before looking up into her almond-colored eyes. "Listen. I'll pack a bag tonight. After my meeting tomorrow, I'll catch a flight to America and meet up with you. We can stay there for Christmas. I know how you love all that silly Santa stuff they do over there."

"What if tomorrow is too late?" she asked, trying to keep tears from forming in her eyes.

"It won't be," he assured. Leaning forward, he kissed the top of her head. "I'll meet up with you. I promise. You don't have anything to worry about." He gave her arm a reassuring squeeze and asked, "Where should I meet you?"

Erika had to swallow before she was able to speak. "L...Lancaster." She took a deep breath, trying to keep from breaking down into tears and making a fool of herself. "Lancaster, Pennsylvania."

A quizzical grin touched his lips. "I've never even heard of it. What's in Lancaster?"

"Farms. It's Amish country."

Tye chuckled as his eyebrows furrowed in confusion. "You want to spend Christmas with the Amish?"

"No. I want to spend the end of the world with you, tucked away in a cabin in the middle of nowhere. I want to be where it's more likely we'll survive."

"Erika," he soothed, though he doubted anything he said would make her feel any better. "You're going to be fine."

"It's not me I'm worried about," she said, voice somber.

He gave her a reproachful look, but chose not to comment. "I'll leave tomorrow and meet you in Lancaster. We'll have a merry time with all your Amish buddies. You'll be begging to come home in no time."

Reaching into her bag, Erika pulled out a brochure on cabin rentals. "I'll be here. Please come find me as soon as you can." She handed him over the packet of information that included the exact cabin she'd be renting and directions to find the place.

Taking the brochure, Tye tucked it into the breast pocket of his jacket. "I give you my word. I'll see you in a couple days. By that point, you'll see how silly this whole end of the world thing is. You'll be wishing we'd gone to Hawaii instead."

"I hope you're right."

"Of course I'm right. When have I ever steered you wrong?" He turned her shoulders to face toward the building. "Now scoot before you miss your plane."

Erika glanced over her shoulder at him and took in his features to commit them to memory just in case this was the last time she ever saw him. "I'll see you in a couple days," she said uncertainly.

With one last troubled look at her fiancé, she forced her feet to move, forced herself to leave him behind. She couldn't make him come with her if he didn't want to. She just had to hope he made it out of Japan in time.

She knew his business meeting was important, that skipping out on it might mean his career. Though she knew all that, she couldn't help but feel he'd chosen his job over her. He was going to die just to prove to his colleagues that he wasn't afraid. It was senseless. He was too dedicated to his job for his own good. She just regretted that she hadn't been able to convince him of as much.

With her head full of regrets and what-ifs, Erika walked through the airport in a blur. She passed through security as if in a daze, her mind not even registering her surroundings. It was lucky she'd flown so many times, because her body went through the motions for her. She made her way to her departure gate on autopilot, her mind a jumble of uncertainty and dread. It wasn't until she got to her gate that she even noticed anything else around her.

Her plane had arrived. It had come in from New York. It was dropping off passengers and returning to the Big Apple. The arriving flight was sparsely filled. A few locals exited the plane into the terminal. Most of the passengers looked like they were returning home from business or vacation. She felt pity for them, but didn't really focus on anyone in particular until near the end of the group. It was a tall, leggy blonde that caught her attention.

The woman was in a hot pink dress that fit snuggly against her thin hips. Her shoes were three-inch stilettos in the same shade of pink. It was the microphone in her hand that had made Erika first take notice.

A man walked backwards in front of the woman with a camera on his shoulder. A news logo was painted on the side of the large camera, advertising them as a New York station.

Erika took a step forward, trying to hear what the woman was saying.

"The ground feels stable enough to me, and no one looks too panicked," the blonde chirped. "Only time will tell if this will be a hoax or a natural disaster of immeasurable proportions." Her voice had become overly dramatized, building additional excitement with her premonition.

Erika thought she might faint. This woman had flown here to witness the nightmare firsthand? What was wrong with her? Before she could process what she was doing, she approached the reporter. "Are you crazy?" she demanded. "Coming here was suicide!"

The woman blinked and laughed uncomfortably at the sudden confrontation. "Excuse me?"

Her voice was a soft tinkle, placing her age at much younger than Erika had first thought. Why, this girl was still a baby. If she'd hit mid-twenties, Erika would be extremely surprised. She was young and impressionable, just the type of person big stations liked to exploit. For a good firsthand view of such a disaster, a news executive would send her into a dangerous situation with the promise of camera time and a promotion. If she lived, they'd deal with the repercussions. If she got good footage of a tragedy, or even better, died in the line of duty, they'd take full advantage of every second of it. That was just the nature of the business.

Staring into the girl's big green eyes, Erika said in a stern voice, "You shouldn't have come here. People are going to die tomorrow. You should turn right back around and go home where it's safer."

The girl tittered nervously, her eyes flicking to the cameraman for support before returning to Erika. "None of this is for real," she said in a conspiratorial whisper. "It's just a silly hoax. Japan isn't really going to sink into the ocean, you know."

"Yes it is." Erika stared at the reporter, intensity in her eyes. She tried to convey with her eyes how serious this situation was going to become, that it wasn't a field trip away from work.

The camera guy cleared his throat, causing the girl to break eye contact. "Nikki, keep her talking. I'm still rolling. This is exactly the stuff the station wants you to get."

The girl took a deep breath before plastering a fake smile across her lips. "You seem concerned over tomorrow's predictions. What do you think is going to happen?"

Erika attempted to avoid being caught on camera, but it was trained on her. She finally gave up and instead focused her gaze on Nikki's. "People are going to die. You're going to be one of them if you don't get out of here."

Nikki's smile faltered, but she managed to ask, "Don't you think you're panicking a bit early? You're fleeing the country before anything even happens."

"By the time something happens, it will be too late,"

Erika said, desperately trying to get through to her. "Do you think they're going to fly everyone out before it sinks? They won't have time. They'll get out the Prime Minister, possibly his cabinet. They aren't going to care about some American reporter. If Japan sinks, you sink with it."

She didn't want to admit it out loud, but it might even be too late to get a flight out as it was. She'd booked her seat and made her plans two months ago, and tickets out of Japan were getting harder to find back then. She could only imagine it would be impossible now, days from the predicted end of the world.

Nikki shot another nervous glance toward the cameraman before a determined look spread across her face and she returned her attention to Erika. "Can—"

Erika cut her off. "I've got to get on that plane. I suggest you try to get a flight out of here as well." With that, she turned and marched away. There wasn't anything more she could do. If people refused to listen, it would be their own faults when something happened.

12

Nagoya, Japan
Nikki Stanton

Nikki waited until the red light that signified the camera was filming flashed off before lowering her microphone and letting out a nervous sigh. "Scott?" she inquired softly to her cameraman. "You don't think she's right, do you?"

Before he could answer, someone suddenly wrapped an arm around her neck from behind and mussed her hair with the knuckles of their other hand. "I told you," said a familiar male voice. "All it took was one crazy fanatic and she's totally freaked out. Girls are so predictable."

Nikki spun around and slapped their equipment manager away from her. "You're such an ass, Tony." She tried to hide her embarrassment behind the harshness of her tone. He was right. She'd let herself get spooked already, something he'd predicted on the plane. It was hard not to feel a little antsy in a city lying directly on the coast when the entire country was predicted to sink.

Not at all offended, Anthony Campbell threw back his head and laughed. "The only reason she's upset is because I'm right. She's freaked out already and we haven't been off the plane ten minutes yet."

The last member of their crew, Pearson Gray, the electronics expert, was the next to begin teasing her. "You wanna go home, Nikki?" he ribbed. "Are you that worried?"

Eyebrows lowering into a glare, she snapped, "I'm fine. I'm more concerned about what my hair looks like after what jerk off did to it." She patted her blonde locks, making sure everything was back in place as Pearson gave a hoot of appreciation at her insult.

"She just called me a jerk off," Tony cackled, sounding more delighted by her jab than he should have been.

Scott lowered his camera to his side and rolled his shoulders as if to ease away the stiffness the heavy equipment had caused. "Forget that chick, all right? She was crazy. Nothing more to it." A devilish grin spread across his lips, making his face look even more handsome than normal. "I know what can help take the edge off of dealing with all these weirdoes." He paused dramatically. "Let's go find a bar."

Cheers from Tony and Pearson met his suggestion.

Nikki was more reluctant to agree to this proposal than the others. "We're supposed to be getting footage," she reminded them.

Scott shot her a persuasive look. "You want good footage? I would think the best place to get that would be a bar. People talk all kind of crazy stuff when they're drunk. You'll get more interesting comments in a bar than anywhere else."

Nikki bit her lip and shifted her weight from one foot to the other. "I don't know..." She knew he was right, of course. People loosened up in a casual environment. She would probably get more from people there than out on the streets bugging commuters because they were chasing a rumor. Professionals wouldn't be caught dead commenting on something they believed to be a hoax. "All right," she finally conceded. "We'll hit the bars." Her surrender was greeted by hoots of approval. She pointed a finger at them in warning. "I'm serious about this project, guys. You'd better get me some good interviews, or I'm dragging you all back to public transportation areas."

With a cry of delight, Tony tugged her toward him and placed a smacking kiss on her cheek. "You're the best, Nik. You won't regret this."

She trudged after them with a laugh, unable to stay grim with their high-spirited attitudes. "I bet I'll be really sorry when I'm forced to haul all your drunk asses into a cab."

"Let's hope so!" Pearson cried merrily.

12

London, England
Hugh Western

Hugh was pacing his loft. His hands were balled into fists at his sides, and his mind was moving a mile a minute. "There has to be a way," he mumbled to himself. "We can't be expected to just take this lying down. We should have a choice."

"Hugh." A soft voice interrupted his ranting.

He could pick that voice out of a crowd. It was a voice he'd come to love more than anything in the world. He tried to push his concerns to the back of his mind, and then turned to face his wife, Elizabeth.

She was standing in the doorway, leaning against the doorframe with a small smile meant just for him. A corner of her mouth twitched upward in amusement at catching him talking to himself.

Hugh returned the smile with absolute fondness, his expression almost embarrassed at her walking in on his ramblings. He studied the way her blonde hair cascaded over her shoulders, the way her green eyes sparkled with happiness at just the mere sight of him.

They'd been married two years, and he still found himself in disbelief that she'd ever agreed to such a thing. Hell, he was surprised she even agreed to go out with him to begin with. He was thirty-six when they met. By that point, he'd pretty much ruled out the idea of marriage. Yet after a four month whirlwind courtship, he'd proposed.

Elizabeth was nine years younger than him, a fact her parents hadn't been thrilled about. Despite their age difference and social pressure from family, they'd been happily married for the past two years. Her parents had even recently made the grudging admission that he was good for their daughter.

The woman of his dreams suddenly pushed away from the doorframe and sauntered toward him, her three-inch heels clicking with every step.

He couldn't help his eyes from straying to the sexy saunter of her hips. She oozed sex appeal. She could snag any man she wanted in her age range, yet she'd chosen him, a mildly successful artist. Working as an attorney, her job was serious and dry. She claimed he lightened her life. Before him, she hadn't known how to relax and enjoy life. She'd been too caught up in business meetings and designer suits.

Upon reaching him, she ran her fingers through the gray hair that had recently been coming in through the brown at his temples and pressed a kiss to the corner of his mouth. "What's for dinner?" she purred as she pulled away.

He cursed softly under his breath. "Dinner. I knew I forgot something."

Elizabeth frowned, concern drawing her eyebrows close together. "Is something wrong? You seem...distracted."

He almost said no, but he knew she'd see through him. "That atom smasher is scheduled to be turned on tomorrow," he admitted, running a hand along the back of his neck as he avoided eye contact.

Her brow smoothed, and she ran a hand along his arm. "Is that what this is about?" she asked in surprise. "I knew you weren't keen on the idea, but I had no clue it was bothering you to this degree."

"Neither did I, but I was just thinking... They turn that thing on tomorrow and the entire planet might be sucked into a black hole. It's a scary thought."

Stepping into his arms, Elizabeth laid her head against Hugh's chest. "I agree with you. It's an extremely scary thought. I'm going to be on edge all day tomorrow." She nuzzled closer. "But you've heard what the reporters have said. It's unlikely that a black hole will be created. And if it does happen, it's more than likely going to be a micro black hole. It will suck up the people in the room, possibly the building, before combusting. The only people who would be killed would be those scientists. They'd deserve it too for trying to play God." She shifted her face to look up at him. "The odds of the entire earth being sucked in are next to nothing. You know that."

Sighing, Hugh nodded his head in agreement. "Yeah, I know. I just don't like that there's even a chance. Taking such a risk should be illegal."

"I agree." Standing on her tiptoes, she grazed a kiss along his jaw. "But until the day comes that they make it illegal, we'll just have to hate them in silence."

"*That's* how issues get solved," he said sarcastically, adding a chuckle to let her know he was only teasing. Pulling back, he gave her a smile, trying to appear less worried than he really was. "How about I take you to dinner at Georgio's? I know how much you love that place."

Her eyes lit with excitement, but she tried to keep her expression uncertain. "That place is so expensive..."

"It's your favorite, and I owe you for not having dinner ready when you got home from work. We rarely ever get to go there. Let me treat you."

A grin of delight spread across her lips. "Okay. That sounds wonderful."

Hugh forced himself to smile in return. Georgio's was a pricey restaurant that had romantic umbrella covered tables on an outside balcony. It was a place where people fell in love, where they'd had their first date actually. He wasn't choosing it because it was his wife's favorite, though. He'd chosen it because it sat across the street from the exact building that held the atom smasher.

Yellowstone National Park
Silver Gate, Montana
Dr. Kyle Phelps

Kyle Phelps looked at the readout in front of him and felt his heart sink into the pit of his stomach. "This can't be right," he said to himself, his voice strained with fear. "It can't be."

"What can't be?" asked his assistant, Ryan Williams, as he bobbed into the room in time to the music that blared from the headphones draped around his neck. Under his white lab coat were faded jeans, and peeking from under the jeans were tattered sneakers. The kid was a genius, but his idea of business casual was somewhat lacking.

"These are the results from this afternoon?" Kyle asked, though he already knew the answer.

"Yeah. The equipment just sent the information into the system fifteen minutes ago. Why? I didn't get a chance to look at them yet. Is there equipment down or something?"

Fearing that his fifty-year-old heart was too old for this kind of shock, Kyle handed the readout to his protégé.

It took Ryan less than thirty seconds to look up at Kyle in horror. "Shit. Holy shit." He scanned the information again. "This is bad, right? Like really bad? What exactly does this mean?"

"By my quick estimate," Kyle stated as he lifted his glasses to massage the bridge of his nose, "it means the volcano sitting under Yellowstone Park will erupt within the next seventy-two hours, possibly sooner than later."

Ryan's hands ran through his shaggy blond hair, and he looked at his mentor with worry in his eyes. "I hate to ask this, but how bad are we talking?"

"If I am correct, in a few days from now, there won't be anything alive within a six hundred mile radius."

Ryan slowed to a stop and sunk into a nearby chair, his face pale. "What can we do to stop it?"

"Nothing," Kyle answered with regret. "There isn't anything we *can* do."

CHAPTER 2

Silver Gate, Montana
December 21st, 2012
Jacob Williams

There was a buzzing noise in his ear, something Jacob couldn't quite place. He pushed the sound to the back of his mind and concentrated on the pitcher in front of him. The game was on the line. It was the bottom of the ninth, two outs, and a full count. This next pitch could make or break his career in professional baseball. He tightened his grip on the bat in his hands and bent his knees. This was it. He needed his full concentration...except the ringing got louder, more persistent.

Jacob suddenly sprang up in bed as reality broke into his dream. He cursed in irritation at the interruption of his sleep. With a glance at the bedside clock, he snatched up his cell phone and saw his older brother's number on the screen. He answered with a snarl. "It's three in the morning."

There was silence for a moment on the other end of the phone, then his brother's voice whispered, "Jacob."

The grave tone of his older brother's voice caused Jacob to sit up and pay attention. If they'd had any other close family, he would suddenly be worried that someone had died. As it was, their parents died in a plane crash when he was four, Ryan seven. Their grandmother had raised them, but she would be dead two years in February. Their grandmother's passing had left him and his brother, Ryan, without any other living family that they knew of. At seventeen, he was more independent than most adults. He still lived with Ryan, but his brother didn't usually bother him much. That's why this early morning wake up came as such a surprise. "Ryan?"

"I don't have long," came his brother's whispered and rushed reply. "They'll be back soon."

"They?" Jacob asked in concern. When Ryan hadn't come home last night, he'd assumed his brother had hooked up with a girl. He was twenty years old and single. That kind of stuff happened. He'd never even considered the possibility that Ryan could be in trouble.

"I need you to promise me something," Ryan said desperately. "Promise me that you'll get out of Silver Gate. Go to the airport and get on the first flight out. You need to get at least six hundred miles away. Get as far south as you can go."

To most people, this request might lead to thoughts that Ryan was in trouble with a bookie or some kind of drug dealer who he didn't want coming after his little brother, but Ryan didn't hang with that type of crowd. Jacob knew him better than that and didn't even consider the ludicrous idea. Plus, the six hundred mile thing was an odd request. Six hundred miles was far for his brother to ask him to go. What could be so important that he needed to drop everything and flee a few states? "Ryan, what's going on?" While he waited for his brother's reply, Jacob hopped out of bed and began throwing clothes into a duffel bag. Though he would like an explanation, he had no problem following orders. Ryan had never led him wrong yet.

"The volcano is going to erupt."

That statement stopped Jacob in his tracks. "The volcano? Like the big one in Yellowstone?"

"Yeah. That one." Ryan sighed on the other end of the line. "Dr. Phelps and I went to the authorities when we discovered what was going to happen. We wanted to get an evacuation started. Instead, they're holding us here like criminals. They say they need more proof before they begin evacuating people and start a panic. They won't let us leave the precinct because they don't want us leaking the information to a news station before we give them concrete proof. They don't understand that there isn't enough time for them to be playing around. That thing is going to erupt and everyone is going to be trapped."

"I'll get out," Jacob promised as he rushed into the bathroom for toiletries. "I'm already mostly packed. What about you though?"

There was a moment of silence on the other end of the line. "I'm going to try to convince them to let us go, but I'll be honest with you. It doesn't look good." Jacob opened his mouth to protest the idea of leaving his brother behind when Ryan interrupted him. "I can accept whatever happens to me as long as I know you got out. This is *my* volcano. I want to make it out of here, but I don't mind going down with it as long as I know you survived." There was another tense silence before Ryan said, "Take care of yourself, Jake. Get somewhere safe."

"I will," Jacob promised. "I want you to try your hardest to get out of there, though."

Before either could say anything more, there were shouts on Ryan's end of the phone. "They're back," Ryan said with fear.

Jacob's fingers tightened around his cell phone when he heard a scuffle and then a grunt from his brother. "Ryan?" he called. "Ryan?" Harsh breathing could be heard from Ryan's end of the connection. Then nothing. The line went dead.

Burlington, Vermont
Peyton Rivers

The sun was still a few hours from rising, but Peyton was in her car, trying to force herself awake. She supposed it was technically Friday morning, but it sure didn't feel like it. She tried unsuccessfully to fight back a yawn as she pulled into the Allison family's driveway.

Peyton was in her junior year of high school. She babysat the Allison's daughter, Melody, on a regular basis. Both Kira and Derek Allison worked long hours, Kira many times out of town. Watching Melody was a normal thing. Being asked to watch her in the middle of the night, not so much.

Peyton climbed out of her car and shuffled blearily up the walk. She didn't even make it halfway up the porch steps before the front door flew open.

Derek Allison, all six-foot-four of him, came racing out of the house. "Thank you so much, Peyton," he said breathlessly.

The Allisons were the only African American family in the neighborhood. It seemed like they went out of their way to be the perfect neighbors, as if to prove they weren't going to be a problem. She thought that was crazy. The Allisons were great. If anyone had a problem with them because they weren't Caucasian, they could stuff it for all she cared.

"I hope your parents aren't too upset that I dragged you out of bed in the middle of the night," he said with a note of concern in his voice.

"I didn't even wake them up," she assured. "I left a note on the refrigerator. I just said you had an emergency at the station and I was going over to watch Melody while you straightened things out. My dad gets up a little after six for work. I'll call his cell phone just in case he misses the note. Don't worry about it, Mr. A. It's not a big deal."

Relief filled his face. "Thank you so much, Peyton. I'll make this worth your time. Hopefully, I won't be gone too long. The equipment went down, but we can pray it's just a fuse or something else easy to fix."

"Get going!" she urged with a laugh. "Melody and I will be fine. You should be worrying about the station instead of us."

He nodded in agreement. As he shook off his concern over leaving his daughter in the middle of the night, he rushed to his car, worrying now about the news equipment.

Peyton watched him leave, waving as he pulled out of the driveway. Once his car disappeared down the road, she turned and made her way into the house. She went directly to the couch and curled up in its thick cushions.

There was no need to wake Melody to let her know she was there. Mr. Allison would have roused his daughter long enough to let her know Peyton was coming over. She might as well let the little girl continue to sleep.

Peyton didn't have to worry about anything until Melody woke up besides calling her own father at six. After setting an alarm on her phone to wake her at six to call her dad, she gave a big yawn and let herself drift off to sleep.

Nagoya, Japan
Nikki Stanton

Nikki was jarred out of her sleep by a loud thumping noise that caused the headboard above her to rattle in protest. She mumbled tiredly and ran a hand over her forehead, unhappy with the abrupt awakening. These time differences killed her. The fact that she'd drank too much didn't help either.

She felt someone shift beside her in the bed, felt bare skin brush against hers, and groaned. She didn't need to look to know who was next to her. Every time she drank, she wound up sleeping with her cameraman, Scott.

Scott was seven years older than her. At thirty-one, he was experienced and dangerous. When she was sober, she knew he was trouble. When she got drunk, she fell victim to that roguish grin and his bright blue eyes. When she was drunk, she liked running her fingers through his dark black hair, liked the feel of his body against hers.

She groaned again. She wasn't drunk anymore. She just had a really bad hangover and was already regretting last night's activities. Well, more like this afternoon's activities. With the time zone difference, they'd been dead on their feet by noon...Nagoya time noon, that is. At home, it would only have been midnight, but they'd been up nearly two days. They'd gotten enough footage for the day and stumbled back to their hotel rooms by one. Now, she guessed it to be late afternoon, maybe close to five, because the sun was starting to set.

Her groaning must have stirred Scott because his hands slid up her waist, searching for her breasts. "Ready for round three?" he asked, voice raspy with sleep and desire.

She slapped his hand away. "Absolutely not." Propping herself up on her elbows, she stared into the silent room. "Did you hear that noise a minute ago?"

"I didn't hear anything," he assured, "but I plan to have you making all kinds of noise in about two minutes."

His hand reached for her again, and she slapped it away for the second time. "Scott, I'm serious. I—" There was a second loud thump, and then the room made a sound as if the floorboards were groaning in objection. "What is that?"

she asked, fear edging into her voice.

He let out a weary sigh and threw the blankets aside. "I'm sure it's nothing, but if it will make you happy, I'll check with the guys and see if they are having any problems."

"Thank you," Nikki said, pulling the blankets tightly around her chest to afford her some modesty, not that she had much left.

"No problem," Scott said with a wink. "I want you relaxed so we can get down to some serious fun."

She pursed her lips and chose not to comment. There wouldn't be anything further happening between them. She'd made that mistake too many times.

As Scott strode to the door that connected her hotel room to the one shared by the men of her crew, she couldn't help but notice that he was naked. It was also blatantly obvious that he was happy to be here, at least his penis was. "Aren't you going to put some pants on?" she asked.

He chuckled, the sound low and manly. "Nah. I don't want any obstacles in the way when I get back. Besides, with all the noise you were making a couple hours ago, they already know what was going on in here." With that, he disappeared into the other room.

As soon as he was out of sight, she let out a sigh and ran her hands through her hair. "Shit." She lowered her face into her hands and took a deep breath.

Scott was going to be disappointed when he got back. There wasn't going to be anything going on that his pants would be getting in the way of. She needed to discourage him and quick.

She was jarred out of her thoughts when there was suddenly another loud thump and the entire room shook. She was sure she heard a scream from somewhere downstairs. She bolted upright with a gasp. "Scott?" she cried out in fear. Another thump, and the glasses on the vanity rattled. "Scott!" she yelled, her voice edging on hysterical. She didn't like this one bit. Something was happening, something bad.

The connecting door flew open and Scott came racing back into her room. He was no longer aroused, and there was a look in his eyes that frightened her. "Get dressed," he ordered.

For him to be telling her to put clothes on, it had to be something dire. His efforts were usually geared at getting her clothes off. "We're sinking, aren't we?" she asked, her worst fears suddenly pressing to the front of her mind.

He grabbed his jeans from the floor and stepped into them, quickly jerking them up. "Not sure," he admitted, "but whatever it is, it isn't good."

Nikki threw the blanket off and scrambled out of bed. She was momentarily disappointed that Scott didn't even take the time to appreciate her nakedness, but terror kicked in as the floor trembled under her feet.

She was barely on her feet before Scott tossed her the dress she'd worn the night before. Forgoing her bra, she shook out the crumpled garment so she could step into it.

"Hurry up," he urged. "Hurry up."

"I'm trying," she informed him as she stepped into the dress. In her haste, her foot got tangled in the fabric and she nearly fell.

Scott's hand grabbed her shoulders to steady her. "Where are your shoes?"

As he swiftly zipped up the back of the dress, Nikki nodded toward the door. "Over there."

Catching sight of the pink heels, Scott shook his head. "You can't run in those. Tell me you brought sneakers."

"Run?" she squeaked. "What are we running from?"

There was suddenly another loud noise and screams could definitely be heard from within the building.

Without needing any more explanation than that, she grabbed her suitcase from the closet and yanked it open. She fumbled inside for a moment, tossing clothing to the floor around her until she came away with a pair of underwear.

Scott grabbed them from her hand as Tony and Pearson rushed into the room. "We don't have time for that. Just find some damn shoes."

Pearson tossed Scott a pair of sneakers.

Scott shoved his feet inside, tying them in record time before yanking Nikki, who'd barely shoved her feet into a pair of shoes, to stand next to him. "We've got to stick together," he said, his hand a vice grip on her arm.

"No kidding," Tony piped in. "It looks like total chaos down there. We get separated, and there's no way we're finding each other again."

Pearson opened the hotel door and peered into the hallway. "We ready for this?"

"No," Scott retorted, "but we don't have much choice." A thought seemed to occur to him, and he ducked back into the room. He grabbed his camera from the table beside the bed where it had been left the night before. He grabbed his laptop bag and tossed it to Pearson. "I'll get whatever footage I can, and we'll just have to send everything to them raw."

Nikki felt her heart clench in her chest. "You're sending everything raw?" A blush crept up her cheeks and she lowered her voice. "What about..." She sent him an angry glare. "Last night you said you would edit out..." She couldn't even finish that horrible sentence. Last night, she'd let him set up his camera and film them having sex. It had been fun and sexy...last night. This morning, it was mortifying even with the promise of it being erased. The thought of it being seen by anyone else was unbearable.

"You think I'm happy about it?" he asked tersely. "We don't have any choice. Once the camera gets so wet, whatever's on it is going to be ruined. I've got to send them what I have when I get opportunities."

"So we're really sinking then?" she asked with a squeak of horror.

"It sure seems that way," Pearson stated matter-of-factly. "Congratulations, you finally get to be a part of a huge story. You're a star."

"And once the stardom from your news coverage dies down, the sex tape will come out and start things anew," Tony piped in wickedly.

Nikki sent Scott an enraged look.

"Look on the bright side, sweetie," Scott said as he trudged toward the door. "We probably won't be alive to know the difference."

That morbid thought made her anger dissipate. "What are we going to do?" she asked with wide, terror-filled eyes.

"Get as far inland as we can. Then we get on the roof of the highest building we see. There isn't much more we can do," Scott instructed.

She nodded, wrapping that idea around her mind. "That's good. It's a good plan. It's better than just sitting around." She edged out into the hallway after that statement, trying to keep herself calm. Any plan was better than sitting around waiting to die.

As they entered the hall, she couldn't help but notice how

abandoned it looked. There hadn't been many people rooming near them. Tourists had become a rare thing with the predicted end of the world and fear of the country sinking. The other handful of foreigners they'd come across were "end of the world" extremists that her crew had been filming for dramatic effect. The extremists tended to stick to the streets, waving around their morbid signs. Most normal people didn't believe the predictions, but they weren't stupid enough to take any chances.

The few rooms that had been occupied were empty, their inhabitants having already abandoned ship. The hallway was deathly silent and dimly lit. It made everything seem unreal, like they were in a horror movie.

Taking a deep breath to calm her nerves, Nikki started toward the elevator.

Scott reached out and grabbed her arm. "Stairs," he instructed. "An elevator is the last place you want to be trapped if there is going to be water rising."

Nikki's eyes widened, and she bobbed her head in frantic agreement, feeling slightly embarrassed for almost breaking one of the most basic rules of an emergency. "Right," she stammered. "You're absolutely right. No elevators. You're so smart."

Scott chuckled and sent her a sideways grin. "Debatable. I plan to send our superiors a very graphic video of us engaging in sexual acts. Ask me in a couple days how smart I am."

"I just hope to be alive in a couple days," Pearson piped up.

"Don't we all," Scott grumbled, nudging Nikki toward the stairs.

Taking a deep breath for bravery, she opened the door and peered into the deserted stairwell. Not an instant later, the ground began to shake, and the building groaned in protest. She was thrown against the door from the violent vibrations happening underfoot. Then the power suddenly went out.

She gripped the edge of the door tightly in her hand, trying not to lose her balance as her world shifted and moved while she was unable to even see what was happening. There was a panicked scream from somewhere below them, and Nikki had to fight not to join in with one of her own. Instead, she bit her lip until she tasted blood, but it was the only thing she could do to keep herself from crying out in alarm. Screaming like a frightened child wasn't going to help anything. It would only make everyone else feel more panicked.

She was starting to fear that the quaking would never end when, just as suddenly as it had started, the trembling underneath of them stopped. She let out the breath she'd been holding in one big whoosh, relieved that at least the ground had stopped shaking. The power was still out, which was terrifying, but at least she could stand upright.

"Is everyone okay?" came Tony's voice in the near darkness.

"I'm fine," Pearson responded, though his voice wavered.

"I'm good," Scott's deep voice assured from next to her.

"Nikki?" Tony asked. "Are you okay?"

She heard his inquiry, but was unable to form the words to tell him she wasn't hurt. She stood trembling in the darkness, feeling near hysterics.

"Nikki?" Tony asked again, concern creeping into his voice.

A hand suddenly grabbed her forearm. She was pulled close against the person's chest, and it was Scott who answered, "She's fine. Just shaken up." He dipped his head, his mouth brushing her ear as he softly instructed, "Hold on." He placed her hand against the waistband of his jeans. "Follow me, okay?"

She nodded. Then, realizing he probably couldn't see her in the dim lighting, she whispered, "Okay."

Scott led them into the darkened stairwell, his arms outstretched from the railing to the far wall to help him keep his balance. "Let's head all the way down to the lobby," he directed, wanting them to have an idea of where they were going. It had to be hard to blindly follow him with their sense of sight cut off.

"How many floors up are we?" Tony asked wearily.

"Twelve," Pearson supplied. "We're lucky. This has been a slow vacation attraction lately. There are thirty-six floors to this thing. We could be at the top."

As Scott continued forward, Nikki clung to him, afraid to let go for even a second. She felt him pull away from the wall and lift his arm toward his eye. Her head snapped up to stare at him, though she could barely see his outline in the dark. "You've got the camera on?" she squeaked in disbelief.

"Yeah. This is what we're here to cover, isn't it? You want to say a few words?" He aimed the camera down toward her, and the screen was filled with her image. Her face looked sickly green from the night vision setting, making the situation even more eerie. "We're not supposed to be covering this," she argued, shaking her head in denial. "We were supposed to be covering a hoax. It was supposed to be a fluff piece."

She moved down a couple more steps and stumbled over something on the landing. She was too afraid to even ask what it was. "The building keeps shaking, and the power just went out." She paused, fingers trembling on the railing. "I can hear people outside screaming. It's...it's really bad here."

The red light flashed off the camera, and the screen went black. "Good job. Powerful stuff, girly." Scott opened a small compartment in the camera and pulled the memory card out. Handing it to Pearson, he ordered, "Send what we have right now to the station. I want to at least get them something."

Pearson nodded and set to work, sliding the memory card into the laptop, working as he maneuvered his way down the steps.

Nikki shot Scott an incredulous look. She couldn't believe he was still worried about getting a story while everyone's lives were in danger.

He ignored her obvious displeasure and continued to press her down the stairs. "The way I see it, if we're going to die, we can either die heroes to our country or just die." He shrugged as if to say it was an easy choice. He then returned his attention to the steps. "We're almost there," he urged. "I've been counting the doors at each landing. Just one more flight."

Together, the group proceeded down, making their way to the ground floor. Once they reached the bottom, Pearson handed back over the memory card and placed his hand on the door that would admit them into the lobby. "We ready?"

"Got choice?" Scott asked darkly. Sliding the memory card back into place, he turned the camera back on and nodded his head toward the door. "Go ahead."

Pearson seemed to collect his nerves. Then he swung the door open.

Nikki took in a sharp breath at the sight of the lobby. It

was a mess. A layer of dust covered the ground from the building being shaken so roughly. Luggage littered the floor. Books, maps, jackets, toiletries, and all other sorts of travel paraphernalia scattered across the ground. The place felt like a graveyard. There wasn't a person in sight, even the staff having abandoned their posts. The absence of people left an unnatural silence in the massive room.

Scott nudged Nikki in front of him and waved his hand, motioning for her to say something about the state of their hotel.

Her eyes darted about for a moment in shock before focusing on the camera. "As you can see," she said with a shaky voice as she motioned behind her, "everyone has fled our hotel. It seems as if they are fearing the worst."

"Good girl," Scott said softly, giving her an encouraging nod.

The nod gave her enough confidence to tiptoe through the lobby toward the front door. "We're going to try to keep everyone as updated as we can," she told the camera. She stepped up to the door, wrapped her fingers around the handle, and took a deep breath. "We're about to enter the streets of Nagoya." She took another deep breath and finally turned her attention away from the camera. She opened the door and looked at the street for the first time. What greeted her was total chaos.

The camera in Scott's hand fell to his side as he surveyed the outside world with shock, only now able to fully see the destruction with the hotel doors flung wide open.

CHAPTER 3

LaGuardia Airport, Flushing Bay
New York, New York
Erika Kimura

Erika had arrived at LaGuardia airport forty minutes ago. Her body was feeling funky from jet lag, and she was stiff from the long flight, but she was here, in the land of opportunity...or more like the land of non-sinkage.

She idly watched bags as they made their way around the carousel in baggage claim. As she waited for hers to appear, her thoughts went to Tye. She silently cursed him for being so stubborn. At the same time, she prayed that he would somehow survive what she feared was about to happen.

Luckily for her, her bags full of non-perishables and emergency supplies appeared quickly, so she didn't have to worry about her fiancé long. Her concerns became fully concentrated on getting to her rental car and starting the long drive to Lancaster. She'd cut the trip too close. She should have been here a week ago.

One thing that was going her way was the weather. There wasn't any snow. It was currently fifty-four degrees in Lancaster, nice for what she understood the normal December weather to be. That would make the drive quicker and easier.

As she rolled her luggage toward the car rental counter, she passed a bar and slowed down at the sound of surprised murmurs from inside. It wasn't the normal, quiet chatter of a bar. It was a more stunned, frightened sound.

Her shoulders tensing, Erika took a step inside. She followed everyone's gaze to the television hanging from the ceiling above the bar and nearly collapsed with shock.

On the screen was the terrified, dirt-streaked reporter she'd spoken to in Nagoya's airport. The caption read "Japan Sinking?" Emergency messages and information scrolled along the bottom of the screen.

Erika grabbed onto a chair when the cameraman pulled

the camera away from the young woman and turned it to the streets. She recognized the area. It was barely ten minutes from her and Tye's apartment.

The streets were a mess, littered with debris and trash. A thin cloud of dust hung in the air, and people ran about in confusion, seemingly without an ounce of organization. It was a nightmare come true.

She tried not to look too closely at any of the people on the screen for fear of seeing someone she knew. She forced herself to look away from the television. Watching this would only frighten her more. She knew she had a rough journey ahead of her and stalling would only make things worse.

Taking a deep breath for courage, she turned and rushed out of the bar. She made a beeline for the rental car counter. She needed to get to Lancaster as soon as possible, because she feared the situation in Japan was only the beginning.

Cairo Egypt
December 20th, 2012
Lilly Singh

Lilly inched her way to the checkout counter of the small café she was at with her muffin and a cup of fruit. She was quick to count out her tally, as she'd studied the money system before she'd even come to Egypt. She was then on her way to one of the outside tables in no time.

The sun was shining, making the weather relatively nice. She'd picked to visit Egypt in December so that she didn't roast in the summer heat. This was probably the best time, temperature wise, to make the trip.

She leaned back in her seat and enjoyed the view. Egypt. She could still barely believe she was here. As she surveyed the area with delight, her eyes landed on a camel and she smiled. She had to ride one of those before she left. She couldn't come to Egypt and not ride a camel.

She returned to her dinner, which her body was still convinced was tomorrow's breakfast. She swore by the time her body figured out the change, it would be time to return home. No matter. It was still an amazing trip even if she did have to continue to eat fruit for dinner and meats for breakfast.

She reached for a piece of fruit, and her eyebrows drew together in confusion as she watched it dance around in her cup. She frowned and glimpsed up at the restaurant. She knew to be cautious with food from other countries, but wiggling fruit was a bit crazy.

Against her leg, the metal frame of the table began to shake and clatter. She looked down at it in confusion, and then shivered as her feet tingled with vibrations coming from the ground.

She glanced up and around, expecting to see some type of animal stampede. Instead, she saw the similarly confused expressions of others nearby. The ground began to tremble more noticeably under her feet, causing the table to rattle against the stone patio it sat on.

Lilly's heart leapt to her throat as she realized these were the beginning tremors of an earthquake. She jumped to her feet, but then froze, uncertain of what she should do now. She'd never been in an earthquake before and didn't have a clue about what to do. Was it safer to be inside or out? She remembered something about getting in a doorway, but that was if you were already inside a building. She wasn't sure if that still applied if you were out in the open.

She shuffled her feet back and forth in nervous indecision as people around her began to scatter. The ground gave a violent shift under her feet and she was forced to grab onto her table to keep herself upright. She felt herself starting to panic as people raced past her. Everyone else seemed to have a plan of action while she just stood there. She felt like a deer frozen in the headlights of an approaching car, and that thought was less than comforting. She'd seen the results of what happened to those deer. Anyone who'd ever driven near a highway had seen those results. She didn't want to be one of those deer.

The ground was quaking constantly now, making her teeth chatter together. She spun in a circle, looking for a sign of what to do, some guidance from the behavior of the others around her. When she reached a full circle, facing the direction in which she'd started, something suddenly slammed into her. She was driven to the ground and something heavy landed on top of her. The air was driven from her lungs and her back roughly hit the stones underneath her.

It took her a moment to catch her breath before she was able to focus and open her eyes. The ground was still trembling beneath her, making her vision waver, but she was able to make out the familiar face above her own. "Tex?" she asked in disbelief. "What the hell are you doing?"

Christian glared down at her for a moment before ducking his head to protect himself as an umbrella from a nearby table crashed to the ground inches from their heads. He stayed silent, his body above hers, protecting her from falling debris and rubble until the earth stopped shaking.

It felt like forever, but the ground finally stabilized underneath them. A soft rumble swept through the street as everything settled itself after being violently shaken.

When the last tremors subsided, he lifted his head and glared at her again. "My name isn't Tex. Stop calling me that. I'm going to get a complex...or I'll start talking with a southern twang, which is something neither of us wants to hear." He climbed to his feet and offered a hand to help her up. "As for what I'm doing, that big chunk of building almost crushed your skull into tiny fragments. I saved your ass by knocking you out of the way. Apparently, you're displeased by this."

Startled into stunned silence, Lilly let him help her to her feet. She stared in shock at the large chunk of stone that lay smashed against the ground where she'd been standing. "Holy crap," she breathed. "Wow."

"Yeah. They'd have been scraping your brains off the patio for a week," Christian agreed.

Lilly's eyes reluctantly slid away from the destructive chunk of stone back to Christian. "That's…wow." She gently touched the back of her head, imagining the damage that would have been done to her. "Thank you." A frightening thought occurred to her, and she spoke aloud before she could stop herself. "I owe you." She grimaced. "I owe you my life."

Christian rolled his eyes in annoyance at the look of horror on her face. "You don't owe me anything. I wasn't looking to get you indebted to me. I just didn't want to watch your brains get smashed into the pavement. I didn't have any ulterior motive behind my actions."

At his offended expression, Lilly softened. "I'm sorry. You're right. Here I should be grateful, and instead, I'm acting all suspicious. I—"

Before she could continue, he interrupted her. "Actually, now that I think of it, there is something you could do for me."

Her mind automatically went to something sexual, and she gave him a look of disgust.

Knowing exactly where her mind went, Christian gave a huff of exasperation. "Not that."

She crossed her arms and stared up at him in annoyance. "What then?"

"Sneak into the pyramids with me."

His statement caught her completely off guard. She stared at him for a moment in silence, trying to find a reasonable explanation for his request. When she could come up with none, she finally asked, "Huh?"

"I know it sounds crazy, but I want you to sneak into one of the pyramids with me."

"It does sound crazy," Lilly agreed. "You can't just break into places around here. They take that kind of stuff seriously. And around here, the punishment isn't just a slap on the wrist.

12

They'll shoot you."

Christian managed to look sheepish and ran a hand along the back of his neck. "It might be worth the risk," he said softly under his breath.

Her mouth dropped open in disbelief. "What? Are you planning on stealing something from a historical monument? You should be ashamed of yourself!"

He frantically waved off her accusation, glancing around to make sure no one had heard her. "No! Of course not!" He took her by the elbow and lowered his voice. "I was just thinking...with this earthquake thing...what if all those predictions about the world ending are true? What if this was just the beginning? What if stuff like this starts happening all over the world? What if this is the start of something really terrible?"

"You mean like the Ancient Mayan predictions?" Lilly asked skeptically. "Really? Someone that's sat through Professor Dayton's lectures can still believe in that nonsense?"

"What if all that nonsense is actually right?" he pressed. "If by some odd chance, things are about to get really bad, the safest place is a structure made out of natural materials. We're at the best in the world."

Lilly shook her head, taking a tiny step away from him. "Nothing is going to happen, Tex. It was an earthquake. They happen. I'm not going to go sneaking into the pyramids over a little scare. I think you're letting your imagination run away with you a bit."

Christian's lips pulled into a frown. "If I'm right, next time, the 'little scare' could mean your life."

She stared at him for a moment without speaking, feeling slightly touched by his concern. Whether his intentions were honorable or not, it didn't change anything. She wasn't about to run off with a stranger to commit a crime, no matter how harmless his reasons.

To his statement, she said, "Well, if you're right, then the joke would be on me." With that, she started to walk away. She got a few steps before she paused and looked over her shoulder. "Thank you for what you did, but..." She couldn't think of how to finish that sentence, so she just shook her head, turned her back on him, and walked away.

London, England
December 21st, 2012
Hugh Western

Hugh was pacing again. He hadn't slept well. He'd spent the majority of the night tossing and turning. All he could think about was that stupid atom smasher. Weeks ago, it had been the furthest thing from his mind. Recently, it had been entering his thoughts more and more often until it started to consume him.

Running his hands through his hair, he continued to tread back and forth across the living room. He wanted to scream. He wanted to pull at his own hair until he stopped obsessing over this, but the more he tried to put it out of his mind, the more persistently it was there. He was even starting to dream about the damn thing. It was like a plague that he couldn't shake.

"Hugh?" a soft voice asked behind him.

He spun to find Elizabeth standing in the doorway, her eyes bleary from sleep.

"What are you doing up?" she asked in surprise. "It's five in the morning."

His hands fell away from his hair and he stared at her guiltily for a moment. "I couldn't sleep," he finally said.

Her eyes flicked to the clock on the wall. "I'm meeting with a client at seven. Since you're up, do you want to make me some coffee while I get in the shower? We can have breakfast together when I get out."

Hugh nodded, barely registering what she was saying. "Sure." Without another word, he turned and trudged into the kitchen. Elizabeth had bought a big, fancy coffeemaker that he'd never learned to use. He didn't much care for coffee anyway. He bypassed it and went for the teakettle instead. Filling it with water, he then set it to boil.

After turning a flame on under the kettle, he leaned back against the counter to stew. He couldn't even fathom how Beth was able to concentrate on getting to work as if this was a regular day. By this time tomorrow, they could all be dead because of a stupid machine.

Elizabeth entered the room as the kettle whistled, making him realize how long he'd been lost in thought. "Tea?" she asked in amusement. "The coffee maker still too advanced for you?"

"Something like that," he mumbled as he turned the flame off under the kettle.

When he turned his back to her, Elizabeth wrapped her arms around his waist. Her hands slid slowly up his chest, nails grazing against his shirt. "We could always skip the tea and do something more fun," she purred in his ear.

Hugh froze, his shoulders tensing, but she didn't seem to notice.

"Sex will start my day off right, and hopefully, it will help you get back to sleep." Her hands slid back down his chest, moving lower and lower until she reached the waistband of his pants.

When her fingers grasped the drawstring of his sweats, Hugh grabbed her hands to halt her. Turning to face his wife, he said the only thing he could. "I'm going to protest them." As soon as he said it, he felt as if a weight had been lifted from his shoulders. This was something he had to do. He wouldn't be able to rest until he did something to publicly show his disapproval of the smasher.

Elizabeth's sultry grin fell at his serious expression, and her hands dropped uncertainly to her sides. "Protest who?" she asked, her voice soft with confusion.

"The scientists who are turning on that atom smasher. I'm going to wait outside the doors until they show up so I can give them a piece of my mind. They have to know that people don't support this. There are bound to be other pro-testors. I want to join them."

Elizabeth blinked up at him, her blue eyes full of concern. "Hugh..."

"I have to do this," he said firmly.

There was a moment of silence before a look of resolve spread across her face. "Then I'm going with you."

He shook his head in protest, his stomach turning at the thought of his delicate wife anywhere near that monstrous machine. "No. I don't want you anywhere near that thing."

Her hands were suddenly on his cheeks. "If the world gets sucked into a black hole, I'm dead anyway. I'd rather be with you when it happens. Plus, this is important to you.

We're in this together. We're a team, Hugh. You and me against the world, right?"

A smile spread slowly across his lips at her support. He thought this was crazy. He could only imagine what she thought, but she was sticking with him despite how ludicrous this whole thing was. That was what made her so utterly perfect in his eyes, her absolute acceptance of him, no matter what he did or said. If that wasn't love, he didn't know what was. "Did I ever tell you that I love you?"

She smiled in return. "Only about a million times, but I wouldn't mind hearing it again."

"I love you," he repeated, leaning in to give her a quick kiss. "Now go dress yourself in some sexy protestor's attire."

Elizabeth gave him a mock salute. "Aye aye, captain. Just give me five minutes to clear my work schedule." With that, she raced back into their bedroom to prepare for their day.

12

Burlington, Vermont
Peyton Rivers

Peyton was startled out of a deep sleep by a booming clap of thunder that echoed through the Allisons' still house. She bolted upright with a little gasp, her heart pounding in her chest. Staring into the near darkness caused by the storm, she tried to catch her breath as she silently told herself that it was just thunder, nothing to be afraid of.

Her eyes shifted to the window next to the television as another clap of thunder tore through the quiet of the early morning. It sounded like quite a storm was building up out there. Shivering from the chilly air brought in through the cracked window by the approaching rain, she snuggled more securely against the couch. She was prepared to stay curled up right where she was until the approaching storm passed through.

In the momentary silence left by the retreating thunder, her cell phone rang, causing her to jump in surprise. Reaching over, Peyton fumbled around on the coffee table until her fingers closed around the annoying loud electronic.

Her gaze slid to the clock. It was only twenty after six. Who could be calling her? She'd already spoken to her father. She couldn't imagine who else would need to talk to her this early.

She looked down at the display on the phone and was surprised to see Derek Allison's cell phone number. The only time he ever called her was when he was running late, but she wasn't expecting him for another few hours. She quickly hit the accept button and raised it to her ear. "Hello?"

"Peyton, thank God," she heard him breathe in relief. "I was so worried."

Her heart leaping to her throat at the fear in his voice, she asked, "What's wrong?" Her fingers tightened around her phone as another clap of thunder sounded in the background, making his apprehension seem even more eerie.

"Have you seen the news?" he asked, voice cautious.

Peyton shook her head, blonde locks falling into her eyes as she said, "No."

"I don't want to scare you, but there are some very extreme things happening across the globe." He paused before asking very softly, "Is Melody awake?"

"No," Peyton informed him, her voice taking on a nervous tone. "She's still in bed."

"I don't want you to repeat any of this to her. I don't want to unnecessarily frighten her..." He trailed off as if he didn't even want to tell Peyton about what had him so troubled. Finally, he cleared his throat and said, "It looks as if Japan might be sinking."

A startled, choking sound escaped her throat. "Japan?" It didn't even seem possible. How could an entire country sink?

"Yes," he confirmed, "Japan." There was a moment of silence before he whispered, "Kira's there."

The gravity of the situation finally sunk in. If what he was saying was true, then Melody's mother was in a lot of danger. "I won't say anything to her," Peyton promised.

"Thank you," Derek breathed. "It might not seem as terrifying coming from her father." Another clap of thunder even closer than the last boomed through the air, causing their connection to go fuzzy. As soon as it cleared, he said, "I'm leaving the station in the hands of the assistant manager. I'm on my way home. Our weather guy said there are some pretty severe storms on the way, which is scary in itself in December. Keep an eye on the Weather Channel until I get home." He quickly added, "And make sure Zeke is inside. He gets freaked out during storms. If he was outside when it started, he won't come back in unless someone goes out for him. He'll just hide out there."

"I'll make sure he's inside," she promised.

Before she could say anything else, Derek hastily said, "I'm on my way."

Peyton heard him disconnect. Tucking her phone into her pocket, she climbed to her feet and hugged her arms across her chest with a little shiver. She hated to admit it, but she was a little freaked out by their conversation. Making her way over to the window, she peeled the curtains back and peered into the gloomy morning light.

The sky was thick with storm clouds and a warning drizzle was falling. The wind had picked up since she'd been here, whipping tree branches roughly against the side of the house.

She let the curtain slide back across the window with a

12

grimace. "I so don't want to have to go out there." Spinning to face the living room, she whistled in an attempt to get the dog's attention. "Zeke!" she called out softly, trying not to wake Melody. "Zeke!"

At the silence that greeted her, she grumbled under her breath. She was going to have to go outside and look for him. She trudged through the kitchen to the back door. She then headed out toward the yard. "Zeke!" She spotted him instantly.

He was cowering under the slide of Melody's swing set. All thirty pounds of puppy sat quivering against the bright yellow plastic.

Zeke looked like he was a mix between a collie and a mastiff. At only four months, he was a massive, cream-colored fur ball. As big as he might be, Zeke was just as terrified as any other puppy his age might be in the midst of a storm. He was quaking, a soft whine escaping his throat.

"I don't even know how you manage to fit through the doggy door anymore," Peyton commented as she inched off the back porch into the drizzle. "You're as big as a horse." Deciding that insulting him wasn't the best approach to getting the puppy inside, she instead made a kissing noise in his direction. "Come on, Zeke," she coaxed. "Come to Peyton."

His ears lifted in response to her encouraging tone. His tail began to wag and he inched forward away from the slide.

"That's a good boy," she praised. "That's a *good* boy." Lightning suddenly lit the sky, and there was a loud crack of thunder. Peyton jumped with a frightening yelp, and Zeke went racing back under the slide.

She shot a longing glance at the safety of the house before her gaze returned to the puppy. She couldn't leave him out here, even if it was fenced in. The quicker she grabbed him, the quicker she could get back inside.

Tiptoeing forward, she made her way toward the dog. The wind was even stronger than a few minutes before, whipping tendrils of hair across her face, making it hard for her to see. She pushed them back and attempted to cajole the dog forward again, but he was too terrified to move.

With a little noise of unease, Peyton continued forward. She was going to have to pull him out from under the slide. The last thing she wanted was to be struggling to get the puppy out from under the slide while a thunderstorm raged over their heads. With a sigh, she moved closer still. She was nearly at his side when there was a loud crash from behind her. With a gasp, she spun to face the house.

Melody stood in the doorway, her pajamas rustling in the harsh winds. It looked as if she'd tried to open the screen door, and the wind had ripped it out of her hand, sending it smashing into the side of the house. Her expression was one of fear as she watched her babysitter anxiously from the doorway. "Peyton," she called out, her small voice barely carrying over the wind, "I'm scared."

Peyton attempted to give her a reassuring look. "It's okay, honey. I'll be there in a second. I'm just getting Zeke." With Melody watching her, she knew she couldn't let on that she was just as nervous about the weather. Spinning back around, she dashed toward the dog and scooped him up into her arms. The rain began to fall harder and lightning flashed on her left, but she ignored it. She kept her focus on Melody and the door to dry safety, tuning out her other surroundings.

When she finally made it back to the house, she pushed Melody inside in front of her. As soon as her feet hit the kitchen floor, she lowered Zeke to the ground. "You need to lose fifteen pounds," she griped.

He just stared up at her, tail wagging happily now that he was inside.

Straightening, she closed and locked the back door. Her eyes then went to Melody. "Did the storm wake you?" she asked gently. She was feeling less shaken now that she was inside and had responsibilities to concentrate on.

Melody nodded her head, the white and pink beads at the end of her braids clicking together. "It's scary outside," she whispered.

"Scary?" Peyton asked as if it was a silly statement. "Nah! All that ruckus is just God bowling. That crashing sound is just him knocking over bowling pins."

Melody glanced out the window skeptically. "God likes to bowl?"

"Of course he does!" Peyton cried in encouragement. "Doesn't everyone?"

Melody bobbed her head reluctantly. "Yeah..." A smile suddenly broke across her face as a thought occurred to her. "I have a SpongeBob bowling ball."

"That is awesome," Peyton informed her. "SpongeBob is

the man." She smiled and guided Melody into the living room where the little girl hopped up onto the sofa.

"So let's check the weather," Peyton said as she flicked on the television and took a seat next to the little girl. "Let's see how long this storm is supposed to last." When she located the weather channel, she was alarmed by the amount of flashing warnings that covered the screen. This was one heck of a storm.

The picture switched to a weatherman who was standing outside somewhere in the downtown area. He was wearing a suit, but it was drenched, clinging to his frame. His hair was plastered to his head, dripping beads of water into his eyes. "The storm is getting pretty bad out here," he informed his viewers. "We've got violent winds that have reached up to sixty-five miles an hour and some very large hail. Conditions have continued to deteriorate. Local—" There was a crackle as his microphone shorted out, and a moment later, the live feed followed, leaving the screen nothing more than fuzzy static.

The footage returned to the news station, and the woman who now dominated the screen said, "It looks like we're having some equipment difficulty with Jim. We'll get back to him in a little while." She motioned to the large green screen behind her on the wall, which showed a map of the area. "As you can see, the storm Jim is in the midst of is picking up speed. It joins the rash outbreak of violent storms sweeping up the northeast coast." Her expression became even grimmer. "There's been an increase in tornadic activity over the past two hours. We've already counted a record twenty-three tornadoes touching down. They haven't lasted long, but they keep popping up on the grid. If you are anywhere on the northeast coast, we recommend you stay indoors and keep away from windows."

Peyton gulped down her fear. She couldn't let Melody know how absolutely terrified she was. Scraped knees and runny noses, she could handle, but tornadoes were beyond her comfort level. She left the television on, but set the remote down. Composing her expression, she turned to Melody. "Maybe we should get you dressed and into a pair of sneakers."

The little girl's eyes widened in distress and she asked, "Why? We're not going outside, are we? That lady said we should stay in here."

"No! No, of course not," Peyton was quick to assure. She couldn't tell Melody that she wanted her in shoes in case the worst was to happen, so instead, she said, "I...I just wanted to see the new Disney princess sneakers you were telling me about on the phone last week."

Melody's face broke into an easy grin as she accepted this answer. "Okay." Hopping off the couch, she took Peyton's hand and began leading her down the hallway toward her bedroom.

There was another deafening crack of thunder. Peyton flinched, but Melody grinned. "Jesus must be having a tournament."

At that innocent comment, Peyton's lip curled into a smile of amusement and some of her tension drained away. It was hard to stay on edge when Melody was so darn cute. A moment later, her anxiety returned as the power suddenly shut off in the house, leaving them in darkness.

CHAPTER 4

Silver Gate, Montana
Dr. Kyle Phelps

Dr. Phelps paced the small jail cell he was being held in, feeling much like a caged animal. "I'm a scientist for heaven's sake, not a criminal," he grumbled quietly to himself.

Looking back on the psychology classes he'd taken in college, he noted how different personalities dealt with fear and uncertainty. Some people took charge while others panicked. Some people sat back and let others handle a situation while some went into denial. Unfortunately, he and Ryan were dealing with the denial group.

Groups that clung to denial often used violence as a way to prove to themselves that they were in control of the situation. Ryan's poor face could attest to that. He was sitting in the corner, his knees pulled up to his chest. His nose was bloody, and his left eye was puffy and bruised.

Kyle gave his protégé a sympathetic look. "Challenging the sheriff wasn't a good idea. You should have just handed over your phone willingly, Ryan. They may not have locked us up in here like this."

Ryan lifted his head to look at his mentor. "What difference does it make if we're locked up here or in an interrogation room? Either way we're being held against our will. At least now I know Jake will be safe."

Kyle nodded his head, unable to argue with that logic. "You're right. They aren't pretending to play nice anymore. It's probably better this way. I was never good at politics." He'd known Ryan was right all along, knew why he'd called his brother the moment he got a chance. Kyle had just wanted to say something, *anything* to break up the eerie silence.

This was the calm before the storm. He could feel it in his bones. He knew things were about to happen and soon, but the only thing he could do was pace his cage. He couldn't get out there and help people. He couldn't convince them it was best to leave their homes and get out of the blast zone. He had been rendered useless.

With a growl of frustration, he stomped over to the steel bars that held him captive. "Let us out of here! There is little precious time left!" he hollered, not for the first time.

The secretary at her desk tried very hard to pretend he wasn't there. She fell into the category of people who sat back and let others take control of a situation. She was dependent upon receiving orders instead of thinking on her own.

"She's not going to listen to you," Ryan said darkly. His eyes flicked to the young blonde woman behind the desk. "Are you, Penny?"

Her shoulders tensed and she pursed her lips. She attempted to cover up her reaction to him by riffling through some paperwork, but it was too late.

Kyle had seen it. "You two know each other?" he asked in disbelief.

"Yeah," Ryan scoffed, "and I can tell you she doesn't question anything her uncle, the big, bad sheriff, tells her. She won't move a muscle unless he commands it."

Penny's hand slammed down onto her desk in anger. "Damn it, Ryan! What would you like me to do? You ran your mouth and got yourself into trouble...like you always do," she added harshly.

"Like I always do," Ryan snapped with distaste in his tone. "Typical," he grumbled under his breath, his frustration with her evident in his tone. Lunging to his feet, he marched toward the bars of the cell. "This is a serious situation! People are going to die. How can you sit there and do nothing about it?"

She visibly shut down her emotions and turned her back on him. "Once Uncle Dave sorts things out, he'll take care of whatever needs to be done."

Ryan made a sound of annoyance and shook the bars in his hands. "Fuck Dave."

Penny whipped back to scowl at him. "Your personal issues—"

"Are irrelevant," he finished. "This isn't a joke, Penny. More people than you can possibly imagine are going to die if we don't get a warning out to them."

"There will be time—"

"There won't be time!" he hollered over the rest of her sentence. "Lava and ash are going to come raining down on us. It will move too fast for anyone to outrun it. Everything will be covered. Even if the lava doesn't burn someone to death, they'll suffocate under the ash."

"There will be time to run," she repeated, but her voice wavered.

"Everything is going to die in a six hundred mile radius of that volcano. There's no escaping that, not at the last second." He shook his head with a small scoffing noise. "Think about that, Penny. Six hundred miles of death. Every person, every animal, every plant is going to die. Everything," he finished.

Penny's resolve seemed to waver. She looked uncertainly over her shoulder as if to make sure her uncle wasn't witnessing this conversation. "I don't know what you want me to do, Ryan," she whispered under her breath before slumping down in her chair with a sigh. "Dave would kill me if..."

Ryan's heart jumped at the possibility of her cooperation. He gripped the bars tightly in his hands and stared imploringly at her. "Listen to me, Penny. I honestly believe we are all in danger. I swear to you." He took a deep breath before saying, "I need you to trust me. I've never lied to you, ever. I swear on my life that I've always been honest with you about everything. Please believe me."

She made a small noise in the back of her throat and looked away.

Kyle held his breath in silence. Whatever the history was between these two, it was either going to help them or hurt them.

When she finally looked back up at Ryan, there were tears glittering in her eyes. "Okay," she said with a little nod of acceptance. "What do you need me to do?"

"Just let us out," Ryan requested. "We aren't going to run. I just want to call a couple news stations. Let me give people some warning, and then I'll walk right back in here and you can lock the door. Dave won't even have to know you did anything. I'll tell him I called out earlier before they confiscated my cell phone."

She stared at him for a moment in silence, her eyes wide with fear and indecision. After what felt like an eternity, she pulled open the drawer of her desk and grabbed a set of keys. Climbing to her feet, she made her way over to the jail cell. Her movements were slow and uncertain, as if she didn't believe she was actually doing this. With her eyes fixed on Ryan's and her fingers trembling, she slid a key into the lock. The latch released with an audible click. Sliding the door open, she took a step back to give him room to come through.

Ryan exited the cell with caution, afraid to startle her into changing her mind. Once he was on the other side of the bars, he placed a hand gently on her shoulder. "Thank you."

"Just do what you have to do," she said with a thick voice. She averted her eyes from his and stepped out of his reach, her hair falling over her face as if in an attempt to hide herself from him.

Ryan gave her a sad, thoughtful look before stepping past her toward the phone on her desk. "You've possibly saved a lot of lives today."

"Let's hope so," she replied, "because I probably just lost my job by doing it."

12

Nagoya, Japan
Nikki Stanton

Nikki stared out into the chaotic streets of Nagoya and balked. She took a step backwards toward the shadowed lobby of their hotel, shaking her head. She couldn't go out there. It was nothing but complete pandemonium outside the safety of the hotel.

Scott was suddenly at her back, pressing a reassuring hand to her waist. "You have to, Nik. If we stay here, we'll all drown. You know that."

She closed her eyes and took a slow breath before nodding her head. "I know." The group couldn't afford for her to be reluctant to follow Scott's instructions because she was frightened. They needed to stick together and move swiftly. It was their only chance of survival. Opening her eyes, she took a step forward and bravely gripped the door handle that would lead them outside. "Just don't let me get separated, okay?" She looked up at him over her shoulder with vulnerable eyes.

Scott gave her his crooked, reassuring grin in return. "I'm with you all the way, babe."

She nodded, relieved by that. She trusted him. Scott had always had her back in the past.

A perverted homeless guy had once groped her during an interview about a mugging the man had witnessed. Scott had grabbed the guy by the shirt and had given him a few idle threats. At least she hoped they'd been idle, because Scott could get in a lot of trouble if he followed through with some of the comments he'd made that day.

There was also the time they'd been covering a trailer park, which had been flooded from spring rain overflowing the nearby creek. One burly guy had gone too far in his jeering comments about her and Scott had punched him.

She could think of a dozen more times where he'd stepped in and played big brother...or perhaps jealous boyfriend.

Her eyebrows rose at that thought. What had made her mind come to that conclusion? Surely she was wrong. Scott was a playboy and the last guy she could picture with a steady woman in his life. If Scott had feelings for her other than sexual, he would have said something a long time ago.

She shook the crazy thought of Scott being boyfriend material off as the ridiculous idea that it was. Besides, it didn't matter why Scott always had her back. The important thing was that she knew he did.

Feeling a little more confident, she stepped out onto the sidewalk. She'd barely made it a couple steps before she was forced to leap back against the side of the hotel as someone nearly barreled into her on their panicked race past. She stayed close to the wall, trying to keep from being trampled.

People seemed to be running aimlessly, their features full of panic.

Scott had to practically yell to be heard over the noise of people's frightened shouts. "Head inland!" he hollered, pointing to their left.

Nikki was relieved that he'd pointed her in the right direction because she didn't have the presence of mind to remember which way was inland. She was so terrified that she could barely remember her own name, let alone directions. Without guidance, she would be running around aimlessly like many of the strangers who filled the streets. Instead, she was able to inch away from the wall and slowly head in the direction Scott had pointed.

Her progress was slow because after every few steps she took, the ground vibrated under her feet. The vibrations were getting worse with each passing minute and with less time in between, causing her heart to jump in fear. She kept her arms out for balance, trying to ignore the cries of fear that sounded around her every time the ground shifted.

Out of the corner of her eye, she could see Scott with his camera raised to his eye. The lens was pointed at her, capturing the challenge that simply crossing the street had become. She didn't know how he was managing to keep himself upright.

The ground thumped again, and this time it was followed by genuine shouts of panicked terror. These screams were different. It wasn't just the fear of a confused, frightened crowd. It was real terror.

The ground shook again, and the screams grew louder.

Scott whipped around, aiming the camera behind them where most of the shouts had come from. He walked backwards down the sidewalk, yet he picked up speed as he moved. "We need to go faster," he said with urgency in his

12

tone.

Nikki spun to see what had him so concerned just as the ground shook again. She twisted her ankle and nearly fell, but managed to see enough to terrify her as she righted herself.

When the ground trembled, it shook nearby buildings enough that large pieces of concrete were falling from the sky. Chunks of the buildings were cracking off from over thirty stories up, falling to the earth with enough force to smash the roof of a car. Glass shattered in the windows of the buildings from the force of the quaking ground.

The sidewalk under her feet shook again and was followed by pebbles raining down around them from the building that rose above their heads.

"Get into the street!" Scott hollered. "Get away from the building!" He gave Nikki a less than gentle shove, causing her to stumble forward.

Tony and Pearson, who had been looking out into the chaos the streets had become with its speeding vehicles and frantic people darting in between, turned to see what the commotion was all about.

Upon seeing the falling brick and concrete smashing into the pavement, Tony raced into the street. His eyes were completely on the buildings instead of the traffic he'd just plunged into.

"Tony, look out!" Nikki cried, cringing as a car swerved around him, missing by inches.

He spun around in surprise to face an oncoming motorcycle.

The man on the motorcycle waved a hand frantically at Tony. He screamed something in Japanese as he motioned Tony to move out of his way. Though there was plenty of time for the man to stop, he didn't even slow down. He continued yelling in Japanese, his arm waving in the air.

His eyes widening, Tony stumbled backwards, trying to get out of the way. He didn't get completely clear, and when the motorcycle zoomed past, it ran over his foot.

Tony gave a holler of pain and nearly collapsed to the ground. He lifted his left foot and clutched it between his hands. "Asshole," he seethed through clenched teeth. Wanting to test the amount of damage that had been done, he gingerly lowered his foot to the ground. This was followed by another growl of agony. "I think it's broken."

Scott cursed under his breath, shooting the retreating motorcycle a glare. To Tony, he said, "We'll help you. Don't worry about it." Over his shoulder, he called, "Pearson, give me a hand!" Moving quickly, he hefted one of Tony's arms over his shoulder, keeping the video camera in his free hand. After a moment of no assistance, he said shortly, "Pearson! I said give me a hand!" When he received no response, he turned toward the younger man with a look of impatience.

Pearson was still standing on the sidewalk, frozen in terror. He watched as the buildings on the next street crumbled apart.

"Pearson!" Scott shouted in warning as the ground gave another violent shake. "Pearson, get off the sidewalk!"

Pearson glanced up at Scott with wide eyes as if finally hearing him, but the warning came too late. He was standing too close to the buildings.

As his friends watched in horror, a chunk of concrete the size of an end table broke away from one of the upper floors of a nearby building. In the mere moments it took to fall, it picked up speed. The concrete came down on Pearson's head with a sickening crack. It crushed him underneath it, snapping bones like twigs. They saw blood gush a second before the stone hit the pavement. Then it connected with sidewalk, sending chips of concrete and dust into the air.

Nikki screamed. She screamed and screamed and screamed until she thought her lungs might burst. While Scott and Tony coughed from the dust and rubble in the air, still she screamed. And when the dust finally cleared, making it easy to see the ruined, bloodied remains of their friend, she broke down into heaving sobs.

12

A Highway Somewhere in New England
Erika Kimura

Rain pounded against the windshield of her rented Jeep, but Erika pressed on. Many cars had pulled to the shoulder of the road and were trying to wait out the storm, but she knew there was no waiting it out. This was just the beginning.

It started with the wind, rain, and hail. Then came the tornadoes. Then the power outages. Already, she'd heard that half of Vermont was without power.

Knowing such a fate was awaiting the rest of the New England states, Erika had stopped at the first gas station she found. She bought gas cans and stocked up on enough fuel to last her the rest of her trip. Having a trunk full of gasoline might not be the safest idea if she crashed, but it guaranteed she wouldn't get stranded. Once more places lost power and tornadoes ripped areas apart, gas stations wouldn't be open anymore. She was taking her chances and traveling with the gas.

As she continued to force her way through the storm, the traffic became more and more scarce. Every once in a while, she would find a car or two pulled off the road, but most had seemed to head to shelter. She shivered at the thought of being trapped in a crowded shopping mall with panicked, wet people when a tornado hit. All those helpless people packed in together with nowhere to go.

She couldn't worry about those nameless people right now. There was nothing she could do to help them. She had to concentrate on helping herself.

The conditions were becoming very hazardous. There were patches of road that hid half an inch of water, the pavement below making it hard to judge the true depths. Erika had found herself hydroplaning on more than one occasion. Even though it was early morning, it was hard to see through the gloom. Dark, angry clouds covered the entire sky, not letting through even the smallest ray of sunlight. A loud clap of thunder sounded, causing Erika to wince.

Leaning forward, she flicked on the radio. The silence was freaking her out. She needed to hear the sound of other people, even if they weren't with her.

Instead of music, a reporter was speaking in a breathless voice. "Along with the rash of storms sweeping up the New England coast, there have been a few other occurrences. Cairo was just hit with an earthquake. Many buildings suffered structural damage. There were quite a few water main breaks in the area. The biggest story, however, is the escalating situation in Japan. Government officials have yet to make a decision on a full evacuation. China has offered what little aid they can afford, but they are preparing for the backlash of this tragedy. They expect massive tidal waves and flooding to be a repercussion of Japan's natural disaster."

With a shiver, Erika leaned forward and flicked off the radio. That wasn't the type of stuff she'd wanted to hear. She wanted something relaxing, like soft rock, not more news of worldwide suffering.

She sat back in her seat, letting out a nervous breath. So Cairo had been hit too. Things were piling up. How much more proof did people need to finally accept that the world as they knew it was about to end.

As she was pondering the effects of the world's late plan of action, a woman came sprinting into the road.

The woman was drenched and ragged-looking. She was waving her arms frantically and hollering inaudibly into the downpour.

Her gut tightening with anxiety, Erika slowed to a stop.

The woman pounded on her window, seemingly on the verge of hysterics.

Erika was quick to roll the window down lest it be broken. "Can I help you?" she asked uncertainly. She was almost afraid to know what had happened to this haggard woman and what she could possibly want.

"My...my husband," the woman sobbed, yanking on the door handle of the vehicle. "We need help, and no one will stop." Her words were barely audible through her hiccupping and tears. "The cars just keep driving by, and he's stuck."

Erika's heart leapt to her throat in concern. "Where is he stuck?"

"In our car," the woman sobbed, "and I can't get him out by myself. He's too heavy, and the water just keeps getting higher."

"Water?" Erika asked with a squeak in her voice. She threw the Jeep into park and began clambering out. "Where

12

is he?"

The woman waved frantically and began moving toward the side of the road. "Down here. We slid off the road, and there's a little pond down there. The car is stuck. Max can't get out."

Erika followed the woman down the hill to the pond. Sure enough, there was a red car in the center, tilted awkwardly where it was sinking into the mud. The driver's side window was open and water was pouring in at an alarming rate.

Inside the car was an unconscious man. His head was tilted back against the headrest and water sloshed about his neck. He looked pale, unhealthily so.

Without a moment's hesitation, Erika jumped into the icy water. She wasn't tall, so the water was nearly to her chest. She ignored the chilly sting and leaned her upper body in the window where the man named Max was trapped. "If we work together, we can get him out," she encouraged. She grabbed the man around the shoulders, and before she even began to pull, she noticed a big problem. "He still has his seatbelt on."

The woman bobbed her head tearfully. "I know. I couldn't get to the buckle. I think it's stuck."

Erika cursed under her breath and pulled herself out of the car. She sloshed as quickly as she could out of the pond, fighting against the water that pushed persistently at her chest. The air she'd found warm earlier now felt bitingly cold. She reached the slope that would take her back up to her car, but only made it a few steps before she began sliding back toward the bottom. The rain had turned the dirt incline into slippery mud. Struggling against nature, Erika slowly began battling her way up the hill.

Below her, the woman began to panic. "Where are you going?" she cried. "Don't leave us! Please! Don't leave him like that!"

Erika was concentrating too hard on getting up the hill to reply. She fought and huffed her way up the muddy slope, scrabbling at grass patches to hoist herself up.

When she reached the top, her knees were caked with mud, and her hair hung limply in her face from the constant downfall of rain. She ignored both of these things as she wrenched her door open on the Jeep.

Yanking her purse toward her, she ripped it open and began fumbling through its contents. Her fingers brushed the item she was looking for and they tightened around it. Pulling the switchblade knife free, she turned and ran back to the hill.

She was moving so fast that her feet slid out from under her. She ended up sliding down the hill on her butt. She came to a stop when she tumbled into the chilly water.

"You didn't leave. You didn't leave," the woman was sobbing over and over again.

Even if she would have wanted to, Erika was unable to respond because water had rushed down her throat. Even as she gagged and choked, she was climbing to her feet and making her way back over to the car, back to Max.

As soon as she reached the window, she flicked a switch on the side of her knife, and a giant blade slid free. She knew it was illegal to carry a switchblade in Pennsylvania, which was her final destination. It was probably illegal to have it here as well, but she'd brought one anyway for situations just like this. In an emergency, she wanted immediate access to a blade.

Leaning back into the car, she began to cut first at the straps across the man's chest, slicing at the top near his ear where the belt wasn't under water. The blade sliced through the strap easily enough, and she reached her arms down to the strap across his lap. This one proved to be more difficult as it was under water. She couldn't see through the murky liquid, and the knife kept slipping away from her target. It took her awhile, much longer than she'd hoped, to cut through the strap, but finally, the man was free. Erika grabbed Max under his armpits and began pulling with all her might. "Help me," she grunted to his wife.

The woman was at Erika's elbow in an instant, helping to pull her husband free of the car.

They both struggled and tugged. They got stuck for a moment trying to squeeze Max's shoulders through the window, but finally managed to pull him clear. The three of them toppled backwards into the water.

Erika continued to move back toward the slope even though her legs felt like jelly. She turned her head to the side to avoid the water that was sloshing against her face, threatening to drown her every time they tugged on Max. She managed to get the man from the car propped up against the muddy incline. Scrambling to her knees, she knelt over him. Her fingers fumbled at his neck, searching for a pulse. She was relieved at finding one almost immediately. It was strong and steady. Once she looked closer, she could see his chest rising and falling as he breathed. Erika leaned back with a laugh of joy. He was going to be okay.

The man's wife joined her in laughter. "We owe you. You saved his life."

Erika waved her off, water splashing from her arm as she moved. "No problem." With a sigh, she sat back against the mucky slope to catch her breath. After a moment, she turned to face the woman and said, "I'm Erika."

The woman smiled. "I'm Emily." She motioned to the unconscious man between them. "This is Max."

"Hello, Emily," Erika greeted. "It's nice to meet you."

Cairo, Egypt
Lilly Singh

Lilly sat on the bed of her hotel room with her cell phone in her lap, staring at the television at a complete loss. She was watching footage that was being sent from some blonde American reporter in Japan. It was complete chaos. The reporter was stumbling through a dark stairwell, her eyes wide and frightened. The walls were trembling, and rubble was raining down around her as she fought to make it out of the building.

In a clip shot by a different reporter somewhere near the coast of Japan, water was rushing onto the streets. It was sweeping away cars and dragging people down with its strong current. Whoever was holding the camera was swept up in the water, and then the video suddenly cut out. It truly looked like the end of the world.

Lilly's gaze lowered to the strip of paper in her lap. It was Christian's phone number, the one he'd given her what felt like a lifetime ago in front of the pyramids. She couldn't believe she was even considering calling him. It was crazy. This wasn't the end of the world. It was just a few very coincidental natural disasters.

Crumpling up the paper, she tossed it to the floor. "I'm letting his craziness get to me. I have got to get that nonsense out of my head." She made a face. "And I've got to stop talking to myself."

She lifted the remote and went to change the channel, but the next comment by the news anchor made her freeze.

"Along with the tragedy in Japan, America's northeast is being hit by severe storms. Twenty-one tornadoes have been spotted. Already eighty-one people have been confirmed dead. Rescue workers say they expect the numbers to be higher, but there are many places they still aren't able to gain access to. The storms don't seem to have any end in sight either, making rescue operations difficult if not impossible."

Lilly lunged from the bed and grabbed the crumpled piece of paper from the floor. Pacing in a tight circle, she punched the numbers into the phone. As the phone rang, she silently berated herself for believing Christian's end of the world hype. That didn't make her believe it any less, though.

On the other end of the line, a male voice picked up. "Hello?"

"Tex?" she asked. She stifled a groan, wanting to kick herself for the way her voice wavered in anxiety.

Christian's unmistakable chuckle followed. "I suppose that's me. I take it this is Lilly."

She nodded even though he couldn't see her and softly said, "Yeah." She barely waited a beat before asking, "Have you seen the news?"

"Yeah," he responded just as quietly. "I did."

"Your idea of sneaking into a pyramid doesn't sound quite so crazy anymore," she said cautiously, afraid to even voice the idea aloud.

"It's safer than just sitting around waiting for things to get worse," he reasoned.

"I suppose it is," she agreed. After a moment of silence, she forced herself to ask, "You wouldn't mind me coming along, would you? The offer still stands?" She held her breath, afraid he'd say no. Hell, afraid he'd say yes. "I did kind of imply that you were crazy," she admitted apologetically, hoping her humility would help her case.

His voice came through the line gentle and amused. "I think I can get over it. Besides, what's the point of surviving the end of the world if you're alone? I'd be delighted for the company."

"Thank you," she breathed. "I'm feeling just a little freaked out right now. You not giving me shit makes things a little easier for me."

"No problem," he said casually. "Now, which hotel are you staying at?"

Lilly bit her lip hesitantly. If she told him, that meant she was really going through with this. She looked at the television, at the warnings scrolling across the screen. There were so many different places in the world being hit with disasters it was hard to keep count. It was getting to be too many to still be a coincidence. With a deep breath, she gave him the name of her hotel. Instantly, she was filled with relief. There was no backing out now.

"You're about twenty minutes from me," Christian informed her. "Give me thirty minutes and I'll be in the lobby."

"You don't have to do that," Lilly argued. "I can meet you

somewhere."

"It's fine. I have most of my stuff ready to go. You'll need to get a bag ready. Grab anything non-perishable you have. It would be nice to have some bottled water and food if we have to hole up for awhile."

Her mind reeled at this statement. Were they seriously discussing this? They were planning to have to hole up like this was the apocalypse. Perhaps it was. "There's a little store in the lobby. I'll buy whatever I can fit into my bag."

"Perfect." There was a moment of silence before he said, "I'll meet you in a half hour."

"A half hour," she repeated. He disconnected, and she let her breath out with a sigh. Lowering herself to the bed, she put her head in her hands. "A half hour...this is crazy." No matter how crazy she thought it might be, she still climbed to her feet and began to pack.

12

Burlington, Vermont
Peyton Rivers

Peyton sat huddled on the couch with a portable DVD player balanced precariously on her knees. She was pretending to watch an episode of iCarly, a children's show Melody was currently obsessed with. She was trying to behave as if everything was fine, at least for Melody's sake. Regardless of her pretenses, she couldn't concentrate on the wacky characters because she was busy listening to the storm raging outside the living room window.

Apparently, Melody couldn't concentrate either, because she was shivering with fear. She was curled up against Peyton's side with a blanket wrapped tightly around herself for protection, but even that childhood comfort didn't seem to be doing its job.

Zeke was on the seat next to them, as close to Peyton as he could get without crawling onto her lap as well.

"I'm scared," Melody whimpered, not for the first time. "I want my daddy."

Peyton brushed a few braids behind the little girl's ear. "He's on his way, sweetie. He should be here very soon."

"I want him here now," Melody demanded stubbornly.

Another crack of thunder sounded and lightning lit the room for a brief moment before they were thrown back into darkness. All three of them jumped, Zeke giving a whine of fear.

"I want him here too," Peyton agreed. Boy, did she want him there. She was getting freaked out, and the weather was only getting worse. Tornadoes were beyond her babysitting expertise. She was feeling out of her depths and yearned for adult guidance.

Thunder sounded again, seemingly right outside the window. All three of them jumped once again, but this time, a comforting noise followed. Peyton's cell phone began ringing, and she was quick to snatch it up. "Hello? Hello?" she called fretfully.

"Peyton!" came Derek's anxious voice. "Thank God."

She let out a relieved sigh. She desperately wanted someone else to be in charge. If Derek was almost home, he could take over responsibility of this terrifying situation.

"I just wanted to make sure you guys were okay," he continued. "How are you holding up?"

Peyton gave a nervous laugh. "We're surviving. We haven't had power since shortly after I got off the phone with you last time, and Melody's a little freaked out. All in all, we're fine. It's pretty rough out there, though."

"Tell me about it," Derek said ruefully. "I'm driving in it now. I'm already on my way home, but I wanted to check up on you guys. I would suggest you stay at our house even after I get back, at least until this storm passes over. You shouldn't be out in this. It's dangerous."

"I agree," she said emphatically. "I don't even want to attempt to drive in that."

The line crackled, and he quickly added, "I will be home in ten minutes. Just sit tight."

"You don't have to worry. We aren't going anywhere," she assured.

"Make sure you stay in the house," Derek advised worriedly. "Don't go out for any reason. Stay away from the windows. This weather is very violent. Don't put yourselves in any unnecessary danger."

"I know, Mr. A," Peyton said with a wry smile. "We won't move from the couch. I promise."

"Good to hear," he said with relief. "I'll be there soon."

Peyton smiled as he disconnected. Tossing her phone to the coffee table, she hugged Melody against her. "That was your dad. He's almost home."

Melody's eyes lit up with joy and her fear seemed to instantly evaporate. "Really?" she asked.

"Really," Peyton assured. "He said he'll be here in ten minutes."

Melody held up ten fingers in front of herself and examined them. "That's not so many."

"Nope. He'll be home before you know it."

12

Burlington, Vermont
Derek Allison

Derek hung up his cell phone, the ball of tension in his gut loosening. Peyton was a dependable girl. She would keep anything bad from happening to Melody until he got there. He knew he could trust her, and he was less than ten minutes away. In fact, he'd already gotten off the highway. There were only a few back roads he needed to take and then he would be home.

Reaching forward, he flicked on the radio. He'd been listening to news reports before he'd called Peyton. The weather was bad, as he could easily attest, but it wasn't out of control. From the sound of things, there were many places far worse off than them at the moment.

"Tornado sightings in the area..." the news reporter said the moment sound came through the speakers.

"Damn," Derek grumbled, his caution suddenly doubling at that statement. He peered warily through the windshield, but it was impossible to see very far through the rain. Small chunks of hail pattered at the glass in front of him, echoing eerily in his ears. Wind whipped at his car, causing it to swerve, but they weren't tornado strength winds. He felt reasonably safe for the time being.

Leaning forward, he snapped off the radio. It was only making him paranoid. Instead, he picked his phone back up and dialed his wife's number. "Come on, Kira," he coaxed. "Pick up."

The phone rang and rang until her voicemail message clicked on. He'd already left several messages, so another one wasn't going to be any more productive than the last.

"Damn it," he swore in agitation. He had a bad feeling in the pit of his stomach. Kira was in serious danger or injured. He didn't even want to think about the worst scenario, which was gnawing at his soul like a parasite. It wasn't like her not to answer. Even if she was in a meeting, she would normally at least shoot him off a quick text message in response.

He looked down at the phone in his hand, his eyes narrowing in accusation. "Ring," he demanded.

Silence answered him.

With a growl of frustration, he chucked the phone onto the passenger seat. It was useless to him.

Returning his eyes to the road, he had just enough time to gasp as the fierce winds threw an entire shed into his path. The shed whipped in front of him, taking up the entirety of the road. He was driving too fast to stop, so instead he tried to avoid it. He yanked his wheel roughly to the left in an attempt to swerve around the wooden obstacle.

Tires screeched, and for a frightening moment, the car careened on two wheels. Then it returned safely to the pavement and Derek whizzed by the shed, part of the wooden door scratching into the paint on the passenger side of his car.

He let out a whooshing breath of relief, glancing in his rearview mirror at the danger he'd narrowly avoided. His relief lasted only the moment it took for his eyes to return to his windshield. He'd veered off the road entirely. He'd avoided the shed by swerving, but he was now speeding toward the side of the wooden bridge overlooking the local creek. He slammed on his brakes but not soon enough.

Taking a gasping breath of fear, Derek watched helplessly as his car crashed through the railing and plummeted into the icy waters below, taking him down into the lethal depths with it.

CHAPTER 5

Silver Gate, Montana
Dr. Kyle Phelps

Kyle Phelps sat on the floor of the holding cell where he and Ryan were currently locked up. His expression was one of calm, though he knew almost certain death loomed ahead of them. They'd gotten their message out to a few news stations. They'd done their part to protect the people directly in the blast zone. There wasn't any more they could do, so stressing over it was pointless.

Ryan was more anxious than his superior. He was pacing the cell like a caged animal, his hands balled aggressively at his sides.

Penny was sitting at her desk, nibbling at a once perfectly manicured nail. She kept shooting fretful glances at Ryan. It was clear in her blue eyes that she didn't know what to do. Not for the first time, she turned toward them, opened her mouth to speak, and then seemed to change her mind. She swiveled back to her desk, turning her back on them as she riffled through paperwork.

When Penny went to speak, Ryan froze, a hopeful expression on his young face. When she spun away, he gave a low growl of frustration and resumed his pacing.

This had been the pattern for the last few hours. Neither was willing to break the silence, but both wanted it to end.

Kyle let out a loud sigh, more annoyed with the standoff than their predicament. "Just talk to each other already," he grumbled tiredly. "We'll all be dead soon. Stop wasting what little time you have left."

Penny blushed and glanced at Ryan.

He sent her a sheepish look in response. "I suppose he's right."

"I suppose." She gave him a small, embarrassed smile.

Ryan gave her an encouraging one in return. "With our history, it does seem silly to just sit here in silence. If we're going to die, we should be able to put the past behind us and go out as friends."

Penny's head dropped to her hands, and she seemed to be trying to collect herself. When she looked up again, her countenance was vulnerable. "I don't want to die, Ryan." She gulped, and her hands quivered with her terror. "I don't want to be burned alive by lava, nor do I want to suffocate in volcanic ash. I took history class in high school. I remember what happened to all those people at Mount Vesuvius. It didn't end well." She glanced at the door before returning her gaze to his and lowering her voice. "If we were to run now, would we still have a chance at surviving?"

"The volcano hasn't erupted yet, so there is possibly still time," Ryan said cautiously. He glanced at Kyle for confirmation.

The older man nodded his head in agreement. "Until it erupts, there is still the possibility. Once it blows, odds become nearly non-existent."

By the expression on her face, it was evident that Penny was going through an internal struggle. She shifted in her seat, anxiously drumming her fingers on the desktop. Finally, with a look of resolve, her eyes locked onto Ryan's. "I think we should make a run for it."

His eyebrows rose in surprise. "Really?" He set her with a serious look. "If you let us out of here, your uncle is going to flip his lid. You have to be prepared to handle that backlash."

She bobbed her head in commitment to the plan, accepting that she was going to piss off her uncle more than she ever had in her life. Though she looked concerned about the thought of it, her determination didn't waver. "I'm not going to stay here to die because he refuses to be reasoned with."

"You have to be certain you are totally dedicated to getting out of here," Ryan cautioned. "We have to run and not look back, no matter what."

Penny's expression filled with resolve, the anxiety over her uncle washing away. "I know that. Pissing people off is better than dying a saint." She grabbed the cell keys from her desk and climbed to her feet. "Besides, who hasn't broken their ex-boyfriend out of jail before?" She gave a strained laugh that slowly eased into something real. "It just fits our history."

Ryan chuckled and leaned his head against the bars of the

cell. "Things never were boring between us. That's for sure."

She smiled and rolled her eyes as she made her way over to the door. "That's for sure," she repeated in agreement.

They stared at each other for a moment through the bars.

Kyle couldn't help but notice the look of affection on Ryan's face. It was a shame it took such a grave situation for him to reconnect with someone he obviously cared a great deal for.

Their sentimental reunion was interrupted by the door across the room flying open. The sheriff himself stormed through the now open doorway. "What the hell is going on around here?" he bellowed. "The local news stations..." He trailed off as his eyes landed on his niece, more importantly, the keys in her hand. "Penny," he growled, voice low and threatening, "what do you think you are doing?"

Penny jumped with a gasp and spun to face her uncle. The keys to the cell dangled from her fingers, letting the sheriff catch her red-handed. "Uncle Dave," she cried, voice laced with guilt.

"I asked what you were doing," he said gruffly, crossing his arms over his barrel of a chest.

Penny looked at the floor, her face flushing with guilt. She took a moment to build up her courage before she returned her gaze to him. "I'm letting them out."

"You're what?" he hollered in disbelief.

She squared her feet, placed her hands on her hips, and stared at him in a way that showed she wasn't about to back down. "What if they're right? They deserve the opportunity to get to safety, just like everyone else did."

"*Did*?" Dave's face turned beet red in anger. "*You're* the reason this is all over the news? You let them contact the local news stations?" he yelled.

Penny's chin lifted in defiance. "People deserved to know." Turning her back on her uncle, she began unlocking the cell. "I'm letting them out and we're leaving. We're making a run for it. I believe them, and I don't want to die here."

Dave stormed toward his niece and grabbed her by the arm. "You don't have the authority—"

The rest of his sentence was drowned out by a loud, booming noise. The ground rumbled and vibrated under their feet.

Penny's eyes widened and she looked to Ryan with horror. "It's starting, isn't it?"

His eyes flicked to Dr. Phelps before returning to her. "I think so."

She gulped and nodded, accepting that. She returned her attention to her uncle. Pulling her arm roughly away from him, she snapped, "Let us go."

Dave's hand dropped away from her, his expression one of shock. "It can't be," he said in obvious denial. The tone of his voice clearly stated he thought it could be, but he was fighting the proof that was currently causing all of their ears to ring in its aftereffect. He looked between Dr. Phelps and Ryan. "It isn't possible."

Kyle scoffed and rolled his eyes as another rumble shook the building. "I think you've got to get past the point of denial. That quaking of the ground is the first stage of a volcano eruption. Hard to ignore, isn't it?"

Dave shot the other man a dirty look, but didn't comment.

Penny watched her uncle for a moment to see if he was going to hinder her any further. When he didn't move, she returned to opening the cell door.

It wasn't until the latch clicked that Dave even looked at her.

"I'm going with Ryan," she told her uncle firmly.

Dave glanced at her, his eyes unfocused as if he couldn't keep his thoughts together. Finally, he nodded and stepped back.

As soon as he was through the cell door, Ryan rushed to Penny's side. It looked as though he might wrap her in a hug, but at the last second, he calmed his approach and put a hand on her shoulder. "We need to get out of here. Now." He didn't bother speaking to Dave. They didn't have time for a thank you or a conversation. They had to get out of here *now* if they wanted even a slim chance at survival.

Penny stepped in close to Ryan as if for protection from the events they were about to face. She looked up at her uncle in concern, her big eyes making her look young and helpless. "Are you coming?"

Dave stared at her for a moment in silence before finally shaking his head. "No. The people in the area who haven't yet evacuated are going to need help. Phone lines are already busy. Odds are they will be down soon. I'll need to start going door to door, reaching out to people who didn't get the message."

Penny inhaled sharply, knowing that meant her uncle was going to be amongst the casualties. She nodded, though, accepting his decision. Her eyes drifted to Kyle next. "What about you?"

Dr. Phelps shook his head, his expression sad. "I'll help the sheriff get people evacuated. I'm going on sixty. I've lived a full life and I've got no family left who depend on me like Ryan does. It's more important that I help try to get families out, people with little children."

Ryan nodded, his expression a mixture of respect and grief.

Kyle bobbed his head in Ryan and Penny's direction. "The two of you get out of here. Go find Jacob."

Ryan nodded again. Reaching forward, he extended a hand to Kyle. "You're a good man. It was a pleasure working for you."

Kyle shook the offered hand vigorously. "You as well, Ryan, on both accounts. Good luck."

Ryan stepped back, swallowing hard as he visibly fought emotions that were clear across his face despite his efforts. He turned to leave when Dave put a hand on his shoulder.

"Take care of Penny," the sheriff requested quietly. "Try to keep her alive as best as you can. I know I've made that job harder with my stubbornness."

Ryan gave a brief nod, his expression one of a man overwhelmed. "I'll do my best, sir."

Kyle realized that his young protégée had just had the world thrust upon his shoulders. He only prayed Ryan was able to handle the pressure and see his promise through.

"Thank you." Dave clapped Ryan on the back before turning to Kyle. "We should get started and fast."

Taking this as a dismissal, Ryan put a hand on Penny's shoulder and led her out of the room. He didn't look back once they hit the hallway.

Kyle knew Ryan's goal now was to get to his brother. He said a quiet prayer under his breath that the young pair met with success.

London, England
Elizabeth Western

"You're going to kill a bunch of people!" Hugh hollered at a woman entering the building that housed the atom smasher. "Who do you think you are playing God?"

The woman stared straight ahead, ignoring his comments. She acted as if she didn't even see him.

As the woman brushed past him and disappeared into the building, Hugh sighed in defeat. "They aren't even acknowledging us."

He ran his hands over his face, and Elizabeth could tell the stress of the past couple hours were giving him a headache. She gave him a look of pity and crossed her arms over her chest. "I'm sorry, Hugh," she said softly. "They're heartless bastards. You knew that already."

"We need to get inside the building," he stated, dropping his hands away from his face and locking his eyes on hers. They were currently on the sidewalk outside the building, surrounded by other protesters. It was cramped and chaotic. "They aren't going to listen to a hundred people screaming at them. What we need is to get inside and talk some sense into them, one on one."

Elizabeth's expression became skeptical. "How do you plan to do that? They've got a police officer at the front desk. He isn't going to let you just waltz on by."

He glanced into the building at the officer, a thoughtful expression on his face. "We can run past him. I just want to get a few words in. By the time he catches us, I'll have said what I want to say."

"He has a gun," Elizabeth pointed out nervously. "What if he just shoots you?"

Hugh made a scoffing noise in the back of his throat. "He isn't going to shoot us. If he shoots unarmed people, he's going to be in a world of trouble." He shrugged. "Besides, if they turn that thing on, we're probably dead anyway. If you ask me, it's worth the risk."

She took a deep, slow breath. "Okay." She glanced at the cop. "I'll help you get inside, but we're not doing this without some semblance of a plan. You run. I'll distract him. That

12

gives us a better chance of getting to the scientists than just hoping to outrun a cop who looks to be in excellent shape."

Hugh nodded, relief filling his eyes. "Thanks, baby." Placing a hand to the back of her neck, he touched his forehead to hers. "I love you."

She smiled and nodded slightly. "I love you too."

Pulling back, he gave her a quick kiss. "Let's go save the world."

She gave him a mock salute. "Will do." With that, she turned and entered the building. She barely made it a few steps into the lobby before the police officer's eyes fixed on her.

He held up a warning hand as he climbed out of his chair. "Ma'am, you can't come in here. You have to stay outside."

She nodded and gave him an apologetic grimace. "I know we're supposed to stay outside, but I've really got to use the little ladies room. Please, it's an emergency." She could tell by the look in his eyes that she was making his job difficult. If he only knew how much she was about to make things difficult, he would be sending her on her way without hesitation.

Still, he didn't budge. "There are a few restaurants across the street. I'm sure they would have no problem letting you use their facilities."

Elizabeth sighed. "Only if you purchase something," she argued, "and I didn't bring my purse. Please, I really have to go. Sir..." She didn't get any farther because Hugh came rushing into the building.

He turned down the hallway to the labs at a sprint.

The officer went to go after him, but Elizabeth stepped in his way. "Sir, I—" When he went to move around her, she purposely got in his way, giving her husband the few precious moments he'd asked for. "Sir, if you would just—"

"Ma'am," he said with impatience, "excuse me." He put a hand on her shoulder and moved her to the side. He then slipped his gun out of its holster and went racing after Hugh.

Seeing the gun, Elizabeth gave up any pretense of just needing to use the restroom and took off after them, her heart in her throat at the sight of the drawn weapon.

Shouts could be heard from a nearby room, and she made a beeline for it. As she got closer, she could hear her husband's voice booming over the others.

"This isn't worth the risk!" he hollered. "You could kill a lot of people!"

"Sir," the officer from the front desk said in warning, "you need to calm down."

Hugh snorted. "I need to just calmly let them destroy our planet? Fat chance."

Elizabeth entered the room in time to see Hugh pull a crowbar from behind his back. It had been tucked into the back of his jeans and hidden under his shirt. She gasped in surprise. She hadn't realized he'd brought a weapon with him.

The officer raised his gun level with Hugh's chest, his expression turning harsh. "Sir, put the weapon down!"

"I should smash the fucking thing!" Hugh yelled, obviously out of control as he waved the crowbar in the direction of the equipment lining the room.

"Sir, please!" the officer hollered. "I do not want to shoot you."

Ignoring him, Hugh raised the crowbar over his head, aiming at the large machine.

Elizabeth sucked in a sharp breath, fear taking over her. She didn't like the idea of the atom smasher either, but Hugh getting hurt over it wouldn't change the minds of these scientists. "Hugh, no! Stop!"

A shot rang out and echoed through the air.

Elizabeth screamed as her husband's body jerked backwards, hitting a table.

The crowbar fell from his hand, clattering against the linoleum floor. One of his hands automatically went to the quickly spreading blood stain on his shirt, and his eyes widened in disbelief. He slumped to the ground, his now bloody hand clinging to the table to keep himself from hitting the floor too roughly. A few tools clattered to the floor as Hugh's fingers slid along the table, leaving a bloody trail behind them.

Elizabeth went to rush forward when the cop put a hand out to stop her. "That's my husband!" she shrieked, shoving roughly past his arm. She dropped to the ground at Hugh's side, her heart pounding frantically in her chest. "Hugh!" She screamed in terror when his eyes rolled back and his head slumped to his chest. "Hugh!" She shook his shoulders, desperately searching for a response.

The officer grabbed the radio clipped to his waist and began urgently requesting a medical crew.

Elizabeth leaned over her downed husband, a sob escaping her throat. "Hugh, open your eyes. Look at me!" Her fin-

12

gers went to his chest as she cautiously examined his wound. Her hands came away sticky with blood after just a tentative perusal.

Another sob escaped her, and she moved her fingers to his neck, fumbling for a pulse. She wasn't a nurse but knew enough to be terrified by the lack of a steady beat. She moved her hands to his chest and pressed down on the area where the majority of the blood seemed to be coming from, trying to keep more from seeping out. "Hugh! Hugh, speak to me," she cried fiercely.

He didn't speak. He didn't even twitch. His face was pale, continuing to lose color with each passing moment.

A horrible realization filled Elizabeth. "He's dying," she cried in horror. She fumbled helplessly with the blood escaping from Hugh's chest. Her gaze lifted feebly to the police officer. "Do something! Help him!" She could feel her husband's life slipping away, and for what, for threatening a stupid machine? Was this machine really more important than Hugh's life?

The officer knelt next to her, but upon searching for a pulse, his expression turned to regret. He looked at her with wide, surprised eyes, as if he couldn't believe what he'd just done. "I...I'm sorry. I didn't mean to..."

Elizabeth sat back onto her buttocks in a daze as she realized that her husband was dead. Minutes ago, they'd been outside. She'd been talking to him so casually, treating it almost as if it was any other day. He'd been alive and vibrant. Now, he was gone.

A woman in a lab coat made a sound of disgust. "Great. Some idiot protester gets himself killed, so now they'll try to stall the project. It's a disgrace."

Elizabeth's head snapped up and she glared at the woman. "Disgrace?" she shrieked in outrage. "*You're* the disgrace. You play God without a single regard to the consequences." She pointed to Hugh's still body. "That is my husband!"

The woman didn't look sympathetic. "I am not letting this push us back," she said stubbornly. "We've invested too much time for you to screw this up for us." Moving forward with determination, she flicked a switch on the complex-looking machine.

Another scientist reached a hand out as if to stop her, but

he was too far away. "We're not fully prepared yet," he said frantically as she began twisting knobs and slamming her palm against buttons. Despite his protests, the machine whirred to life.

Elizabeth ignored it, her attention fully on Hugh. She whimpered feebly and clutched at the sleeve of his shirt.

He was still warm, but the essence that made him who he was had left him.

Realizing this, Elizabeth sobbed harder. "Hugh, I need you," she said through tears. "You can't be gone."

It wasn't until she heard a cry of alarm from one of the scientists that she looked up from her fallen mate.

"I don't think it's supposed to be doing this," the male scientist said anxiously.

An instant later, a black spot appeared in the air. It continued to grow, getting alarmingly closer and closer to everyone.

Elizabeth's eyes widened. "Is that..." Before she could even finish her sentence, the black space rapidly expanded, pulling in anything and everything it touched.

It yanked in the now screaming female scientist and then her male partner.

Elizabeth felt as if she couldn't breathe. Her eyes lifted in horror to the police officer's.

His mouth gaped in disbelief as their surroundings were sucked into the newly created black hole.

Elizabeth felt pain race through her body. It felt as if every bone was being crushed to bits as she was pulled toward the black void. She attempted to scream, clinging to her dead husband's body as she and the officer were sucked in. Though she tried to scream, it was as if her lungs had been crushed and were no longer able to breathe in the air necessary to allow her to make such a noise. Instead, her mouth simply opened in a wordless cry as her body burst with pain.

Walls were being torn from their frames. Support beams were ripped from the structure. Then suddenly, there was a loud bang as the hole burst. It disappeared, taking its victims with it.

The micro black hole was gone, but it had taken the entire room with it before burning out. The floor was missing in places, causing furniture to collapse through the flimsy remains. It fell to the underground parking garage below, de-stroying vehicles that were unfortunate enough to be parked underneath. The sound of shattering glass filled the air as windshields smashed and windows broke. Thick dust filled the air as the small section of building collapsed in on itself.

Car alarms wailed and beeped, echoing off the cement walls. Rubble continued to fall, crashing loudly to the ground and breaking with resounding cracks. Despite the racket, the screams of those trapped below still rose above the din.

Nagoya, Japan
Nikki Stanton

Nikki was still crying over Pearson's mangled body. She wanted to bend down and cradle him in her arms, but there was just so much blood. She was worried if she touched him, he might fall to pieces. Instead, she hovered over him and sobbed. As she wiped the back of her hand across the tears spilling down her cheeks, arms wrapped around her waist.

"We have to go," Scott said gently, his lips next to her ear.

When he tried to guide her away from Pearson, Nikki screamed and fought against him. "Let go of me!" she yelled hysterically. "Let go of me!" When she yanked away from him, her shoe sank into the puddle of blood surrounding her dead friend. She jerked her foot away, the bloody sneaker print where she stepped next drawing another wracking sob from deep within her chest.

"We have to go. *Now*," Scott said forcefully as he tightened his grip on her waist.

"I'm not leaving him!" she screamed, fighting desperately to get free of Scott's restraining arms. He spun her to face him, and Nikki struggled even harder. "You filmed it!" she accused with a screech. "How dare you film it!" She punched her fists angrily against his chest as tears blurred her vision.

"I'm sorry!" Scott took her face in his hands, forcing her to look at him. "He's gone. He's dead, Nikki. I can't change that or the fact that I caught it on tape. I'm sorry I wasn't able to get to him in time. Pearson's dead. If we don't get out of here, we're going to be dead too."

This seemed to snap her back into survival mode. "I don't want to die," she whispered in fear.

"Then let's get out of here," Scott encouraged. He took her small hand in his and directed her toward the spot where Tony was waiting, drawing her gaze away from the sickening sight of Pearson's demise. "Help me with him."

Tony was leaning heavily against a car, trying not to look at Pearson, but his eyes kept straying to their dead companion.

Seeing the pain and uncertainty on Tony's face, Nikki bobbed her head, tears making tracks in the dirt on her face.

12

Following Scott's lead, she hooked Tony's right arm over her left shoulder to help take the weight off his injured foot.

Slowly, the group began to inch forward. They had to move unhurriedly to avoid the worst of the dangerous mob and falling debris. Besides, with Tony's injury, they were breathless from exertion even at their sluggish pace.

Nikki glanced down at Tony's foot as they shuffled along.

It was smashed in the center, looking unbearably painful. There was no doubt that it was broken in multiple places. Despite this, he attempted to put weight on it again to speed up their progress and ended up hollering in agony. "This isn't going to happen. I'm sorry, guys."

"It's okay," Scott reassured, trying not to sound as concerned as he obviously felt. "We can help you. We'll still get there..." He trailed off as the ground began to shake. Whatever he'd been saying was drowned out by screams of panic.

As the ground trembled beneath their feet, car alarms started wailing like sirens. Dust began filling the air, making it impossible to see.

Nikki choked on the air, coughing roughly against the dirt in the back of her throat.

Somewhere to their left, a building collapsed entirely. It looked to be some type of religious building. The people inside who had been praying for their lives came rushing out in a blind panic. They pushed and shoved, desperate to get away from the falling remains of their fallen sanctuary.

Unable to see through the dust, the panicked crowd rushed into the street. They slammed into Nikki, Scott, and Tony without even hesitating.

Nikki was forced backwards a step as someone ran straight into her. Another person hit her before the first person was fully past, and she was wrenched away from Tony. A third person smashed into her, and she nearly fell over. Before she realized it, she was swept up into the crowd.

Shouts and cries sounded in her ears. People were yelling in a language she didn't understand, tears streaming down dirty faces as they searched for loved ones or frantically tried to get away from the destruction around them.

Nikki felt panic well up inside of her. She was suddenly alone in an unfamiliar place with the world falling apart around her. "Scott!" she screamed in terror. "Scott!" She could barely hear herself through the chaos. She didn't know how he was supposed to be able to.

She was jostled and shoved. She spun in a confused circle, unable to tell where she was even going anymore.

An unfamiliar man grabbed her shoulders and began speaking to her in Japanese.

"I...I don't understand you. I'm sorry," she mumbled, trying to wriggle out of his hold without appearing rude.

The man tightened his grip and shook her, his expression turning angry. He began screaming, his tone accusatory. Spittle sprayed from his mouth to hit her in the face.

"Let me go," Nikki pleaded, squirming to break free of his grasp.

The man either ignored her or didn't understand. He continued to grip her shoulders, his bony fingers digging into her flesh until his knuckles turned pale from the effort.

A sound of fear escaped her at the pain from his viselike grip. "You're hurting me!" She struggled in earnest, trying to break away from the angry man. "Stop it," she screamed, voice turning shrill. "Let go!"

A fist suddenly shot out and hit the man in the jaw. He stumbled backwards, head snapping back with the force. Instantaneously, blood poured from his mouth, clinging grotesquely to his teeth. It ran down his chin and dribbled onto his shirt. Despite this, he recovered quickly. He turned and ran off, blending into the crowd.

Nikki spun to see who had come to her rescue. She was amazed but not surprised to find Scott standing next to her. Scott, her savior, had come to her rescue once again.

Before she could even open her mouth to speak, he grabbed her and hauled her up against his chest. His lips crushed against hers, his kiss forceful.

She squeaked in surprise, caught off guard by his sudden actions. Before she could decide whether she was pleased about his stolen kiss or not, he pulled back.

"Don't you ever scare me like that again," he growled.

Nikki's fingers grazed her lips, confusion written on her face. "Scott?"

"I love you, Nikki," he confessed. "Don't you get that?"

Her eyes widened and her mouth gaped open in surprise. "Wh...what?" Of all the things he could have said to her in that moment, a confession of love was one of the least expected.

12

"I love you," he repeated. "Why else would I come on this death mission?"

"I thought you didn't believe in this end of the world stuff," Nikki said in confusion. "You've always scoffed at it."

He shook his head with an almost angry grunt. "I lied. I did think this was a possibility. Had I been a braver man, I would have told you as much. I would have convinced you to stay home. I would have told you months ago how I felt about you. Instead, I took the coward's way out. I avoided my feelings and followed you halfway across the globe to keep an eye on you." He shook his head again. "Hell, the only way I ever got the nerve to even make a move on you was if I got completely smashed. There was no way I would have been able to confess my undying love and convince you to stay home. I knew that. It would have sounded ridiculous. It sounds ridiculous *now*."

"Scott," Nikki started, but he pressed a finger to her lips, silencing her.

"Don't," he said desperately. "If you don't feel the same way about me, I don't want to know. We're probably going to die before this day finishes, and I'd rather die thinking it was for a reason."

Nikki stared up at Scott, her Scott. His normal *man's man* attitude was nowhere to be found. His face was open and vulnerable. He'd put his heart out for her. He'd risked his life for her. Overcome with emotion, she grabbed the front of his shirt in her fist. She then pulled his mouth down to hers, kissing him with enough force to bruise.

He pulled back, caution in his eyes. "Nikki, I—"

Her gaze held steady with his. "Scott, shut up." She pulled his mouth to hers again, silencing any further doubts. When he finally returned her kiss, it was with an intensity that had her tingling all the way down to her toes.

His arms wrapped around her back and he held her tightly against his chest. His lips parted hers, fighting against her for dominance. There was more fire in this kiss than any from their repeated one night stands.

When they finally parted, she was breathless. She stared up at him as if seeing him for the first time.

With a crooked smile, he leaned in and gave her a gentle kiss to bring them down from the intensity of the last one. "We need to get back to Tony. I left him propped up against an overturned car when you got separated. He's probably freaking out right now. We have to get back to him and keep moving."

Nikki nodded in agreement, trying to ignore the frantic pounding of her heart. As much as she would like to, they didn't have time to explore their newfound feelings. They had to keep moving or die.

Scott took her hand, clenching it tightly in his own. As a unit, they began wading their way through confused and rattled people. It took a few minutes because they were moving against the flow of traffic, but they finally reached Tony's side.

"It's about time," Tony griped as they helped him away from the overturned car he was leaning against. "I thought you'd abandoned me." His tone was teasing, but there was relief underneath, relief that Scott had located Nikki, relief that he was no longer alone.

Scott moved them forward, helping Tony hop along. "We would never abandon you. We're a team, and teams stick together. Now let's find a way to get the hell out of this country."

Denver, Colorado
Jacob Williams

Jacob had booked a flight to Arizona, Phoenix to be specific. He never made it. The flight was diverted, making an emergency landing in Denver.

Apparently, Ryan had been right. In the few hours since their conversation, all hell had broken loose. All flights nationwide were grounded, perhaps globally. People were rushing about in a panic, trying to secure one of the quickly dwindling number of rental cars.

Seeing as he'd picked a random location to begin with, Jacob wasn't all that frantic to get out of Denver. This would do as well as anywhere else. He was more concerned with getting in touch with his brother. He'd called Ryan before takeoff, but never received an answer.

He pulled his phone out now, hoping for but not expecting an answer. The phone rang a few times before someone picked up the other line. The female voice that answered threw him off. "H...Hello?" he asked in confusion. "Does this phone belong to Ryan Williams?"

"Jake!" the woman cried in obvious delight. "It's Penny. I'm with Ryan."

Jacob's initial reaction was shock at hearing his brother's ex-girlfriend, but he then let out a sigh of relief. "Penny! Thank God! Are you guys okay? It's a madhouse here."

"We're...um...well, we're okay. We're trying to get out of Montana." She gave a sudden sharp gasp and then gave a holler of fear. "Ryan! Look out!" She cursed under her breath, the aggravation directed, Jake would assume, at his sibling. "Your brother is driving like a crazy man."

Jacob waited patiently while she chastised Ryan.

"It's a wonder I didn't want you on the phone," she griped. "Your driving skills are terrible enough without trying to hold a phone conversation at the same time." Her attention swiftly returned to Jacob. "We're surviving at this point, which is a lot more than some people can say." She took a shaky breath. "It is total chaos here. I'm surprised you were able to get through to us. We've been trying to call you for hours, but the lines have been full." She mumbled for him to hold on a minute, and then she was listening to something Ryan was saying.

Jacob could hear his brother's voice in the background. It was a soft murmur that he found comforting. Just the sound of Ryan's voice had the tension easing out of his shoulders, as did the delicate cadence of Penny's.

Jacob had always liked Penny. She'd always been kind to the both of them. She was funny, and she never treated him like the annoying tag along little brother he'd been.

Penny had understood that Ryan was his guardian. She'd never once complained about it. She'd even stocked the fridge with his favorite foods a couple times when Ryan had been strapped for cash.

The fact that she was gorgeous didn't hurt either. With bouncy, short blonde hair and legs longer than any woman's he knew, she was nice to look at. Jacob would guiltily admit he'd checked out his brother's girlfriend on more than one occasion. He was almost certain she'd caught him a couple times, but she never called him on it. He never meant anything by it, and she knew that most of the time he looked at her like she was a big sister.

She'd been perfect for them, but something went wrong. He knew it involved her uncle, but Ryan had never given him the details. Whatever the reason, Jacob missed her being around. It was damn good to hear from her.

"Jake," Penny said, breaking him out of his trip down memory lane, "Ryan wants to know where you are."

Blowing his breath out with an anxious huff, Jacob perused the people around him, noting the apprehension was starting to intensify as people were being turned away from the rental car counters empty-handed. "I'm at Denver International."

Penny reiterated this to Ryan, being the middle man of the conversation. "Your brother says to stay where you are. Get a hotel room and lock yourself in. Apparently, there is more going on than just a volcano."

Jacob observed the frantic people as he tried to inch his way toward the hotel without drawing attention to himself. In times of crisis, people could get violent and unreasonable. He wanted to lie as low as possible in case that happened. "Apparently," he said dryly.

Penny continued on, her voice quivering with distress.

"Ryan says we'll come to you."

She yipped in fear, and Jacob heard the squeal of tires followed by a car horn blaring.

"We'll be there, Jake," she rushed out breathlessly. "Just stay put. It's not safe out here." With that, she disconnected.

Jacob watched the nearly hysterical people trying to leave the airport. "No kidding," he mumbled. With one last look at the growing mob, he pushed into the hotel that was attached to the airport.

At first sight of the packed lobby, he feared he might not be able to get a room. There was a group of people pressing in against one of the desks being manned by a hotel employee. His anxiety ebbed when he realized it was the checkout counter.

People were pushing and shoving one another in an attempt to get the attention of the woman working the desk.

One man near the middle of the line turned to the woman next to him and said, "Screw this. We're leaving. They can charge us an extra night, ban us from using the hotel again, whatever. I'm not standing around in this line while all hell is breaking loose outside." He grabbed the woman's hand and left the line, heading out to the parking lot.

Upon seeing this, others in the riled up crowd began to follow suit.

The harried desk clerk desperately tried to keep things under control, but it was clearly a useless attempt.

Shooting her a sympathetic look, Jacob made his way over to the check-in counter. Unlike checkout, this desk was void of people. Apparently, no one wanted to stick around for the apocalypse.

As he approached the desk, Jacob could see the check-in clerk. She was standing in the doorway to the hotel offices just behind her counter with a frightened look on her face.

She stared at the rowdy crowd, her hand fluttering nervously against her throat. When her eyes landed on Jacob, she stumbled a little on her heels before making her way over. "Ch...checkout is at the other counter," she informed him cautiously.

Jacob took in her overwhelmed expression with pity.

She looked to be around his age, early twenties. Her strawberry blonde hair was pinned back, the loose curls falling in a wave over her shoulder. Her large green eyes were made even bigger by her fear.

Had this been a normal day, he would have probably hit on her. Today, he was just trying to keep her from freaking out long enough for him to get a room. Glancing at her nametag, he gave her an easy, friendly smile. "Actually, Molly, I'm checking in. I need a place to crash for a couple nights."

"Oh!" she said in surprise. She made her way to the desk and eyed him from head to toe. When she searched him, she didn't seem to notice his jet black hair or brilliant blue eyes. Instead, she seemed to be searching him warily, waiting for a trick.

Jacob upped the wattage of his smile, then realizing he might freak her out even more with his happiness during a national crisis, brought his expression down a notch. "I'm meeting family here," he explained. "Seeing as how all flights are grounded, I may be waiting awhile."

Relief filled her eyes at his explanation. "Well, let me get you set up with a room then." She pressed a few keys on the computer. "How many days…" She trailed off and lifted her eyes to him in uncertainty. "I suppose there's no way to know, is there?"

He gave her a weak smile, his thoughts turning grim and his stomach turning with unease. "Just put me down indefinitely." He pulled his emergency credit card from his back pocket and handed it to her. "My brother *so* better be paying this bill."

Molly finally rewarded him with a small smile. "What are brothers for?"

As she handed over a room key, Jacob snorted in amusement. His brother had gotten him out of Montana before the whole state turned into a fiery ball of carnage. Ryan was good for a whole hell of a lot.

His gaze lifted to the television in the corner. Alerts and warnings flashed across the screen. The volcano, he knew about. It surprised him to see the news reports about the tornadoes in New England, the earthquakes in Egypt, and the emergency in Japan. He didn't know the situation outside, but from the reaction of the hotel guests, he doubted it was good. He'd had no clue things were this bad, and here he was in Denver, an unfamiliar place that was obviously having issues of its own. "My brother helped me out of the fire by

12

tossing me into the frying pan," he mused.

On the clerk's questioning look, he shook his head. It was too complicated to explain. "Thanks for the room. I'll try not to keep the neighbors up," he said dryly. With that, he went to leave but stopped in his tracks and turned to face her. "Listen, if you start to feel a little freaked out and need someone to talk to, I'll just be upstairs worrying myself into having stomach ulcers until my brother gets here. Feel free to stop by. Talking with someone might do you some good."

On her nod, he trudged away, more worried about his brother than he'd ever been in his life.

A Few Miles outside of Lancaster, Pennsylvania
Erika Kimura

Despite the fact that she was driving through weather that was unsettling, not to mention hazardous, Erika's outlook on life was quite positive. "We're only a couple of miles away," she said in excitement as she caught sight of a road sign through the pouring rain.

Emily bounced excitedly in the passenger seat. "It is so nice of you to let us join you at your cabin. I don't know what we would have done without your help."

"I know I'd be dead if it wasn't for you," Max's husky voice came from the backseat.

Erika glanced at him in the rearview mirror.

Though his shaggy hair was a mess and hanging in his face, some of the color had begun to return to his cheeks. In just a few short hours, he was looking unbelievably better. His throat was still raw from inhaling some of the murky lake water, but there didn't seem to be any other lasting effects.

"I did what anyone else would have," she said reasonably.

"No," Emily argued, shaking her head of brown, bouncy curls. "That isn't true. People kept driving past me. No one would stop." Her voice broke with the emotion of her past terror. "I thought Max was going to die."

Erika's grip tightened on the steering wheel, her fingers trembling in anger at the lack of compassion shown by her fellow man to these two sweet people. "He didn't die. Max is alive, and that's all that matters."

Emily turned in her seat to smile at Max. "You're right. We're still together. That's all that matters." She stretched out for her husband's hand, leaning between the two front seats to reach him better. At that moment, a large tree on the side of the road came crashing down in front of their van.

Erika barely had time to scream out a warning to her passengers as she slammed on the brakes. The tires spun out due to the layer of rain that spread across the pavement. The vehicle spun sideways and hit the massive tree. The van rolled over the obstruction, landed on its roof, and slid across the asphalt on the other side.

Erika could barely comprehend what was going on as confusing shapes whirled in front of her eyes. One minute, they were driving; the next they were upside down, screeching across the road amidst sparks.

After what felt like an eternity, they came to a sliding stop. The sound of rain pounding against the underbelly of the vehicle made an odd, tinny noise that made Erika's ears hurt. She was still having trouble figuring out what exactly was happening, her reactions dulled by shock. Every inch of her body hurt. Her vision swam in and out as if she might lose consciousness.

Groaning, she shifted in her seat. That was when she realized she was hanging upside down, held suspended in the air by her seatbelt. Blood was rushing to her head, giving her one of the worst headaches she'd ever experienced in her life. Blood was running from a gash in her forehead, plunking against the roof of the van as it dripped.

She groaned again, trying to orient herself. "Max?" she croaked out weakly. "Emily?" Her trembling hand reached down to the buckle of the seatbelt, and she pushed the release button. She cringed in anticipation for the impact, and then hissed in pain when her shoulder hit the hard roof. "Emily?" she repeated.

As her senses slowly returned, Erika remembered that Max hadn't been wearing a seatbelt. She felt sick to her stomach as she envisioned the large, dark shape that she recalled sailing past her during the crash.

Fear pulsed through Erika as she squeezed and crawled her way through her shattered window to safety. Blood was running into her eyes, making it nearly impossible to see. She finally found her way onto the road, scraping her already bleeding palms on glass that littered the pavement. "Emily?" she croaked out hoarsely. "Max?" She could barely hear her own voice over the whipping wind and lashing rain. It had to be impossible for the others to hear her.

Squinting through the downpour, she peered in the direction Max had been thrown when they'd initially hit the tree. The impact had sent him sailing through the windshield moments before they'd started turning end over end. To her disbelief, she saw movement from a crumpled form on the ground. He was alive!

She tried climbing to her feet in an attempt to run to him, but collapsed almost instantly. She finally settled on half-crawling, her fingertips touching the ground as she struggled to make her way to his side.

"Max!" When she finally reached him, she collapsed to her knees next to his still hunched form. "Max, are you okay?" Though she'd only met him a few short hours ago, Erika cared about this man. He felt like family, being one of the only two people in this country she was on a first name basis with. Gently, she helped him roll to his side and sit up. She was unable to keep from wincing when he violently coughed up rain water.

There was a large scrape on his forearm that was bloody where the skin had been ripped away. As he shifted on the ground, he hissed and grabbed his right shoulder, but it didn't appear to be broken. His cargo pants were torn on both knees and the skin that was exposed was raw, but he didn't seem to have any major injuries, a miracle in itself. "I hurt," he said gruffly, "but I'll live."

He coughed again and lowered his head to protect his face from the rain. His thick hair hung down into his eyes, but he didn't even attempt to brush it back. "Where's Emily?" he asked hoarsely.

Erika shook her head, water spraying out from her hair. "I don't know. I haven't found her yet."

Fear filled his eyes and Max struggled to his feet. "I have to find her." He stumbled through the storm looking like a man who'd had too much to drink. "Emily!" he hollered, staggering toward the car. "Emily!"

Erika scrambled unsteadily after him as fast as her ex-hausted legs could manage, struggling to keep up. The wind picked up speed, howling as it whipped through the nearby trees. It struck at the front of her body, reducing her momentum with its force.

Trees groaned as the wind tested their durability, causing a frightening thought to occur to her. The tornadoes. They were popping up everywhere, destroying everything in their paths. "Max," she practically whispered, as if the weather could listen in on her concerns. "I think we should hurry."

Max ignored her as he approached the car. "Emily!" he yelled, the wind eerily carrying his voice. "Emily!" Then suddenly, he broke off with a guttural cry of anguish.

12

She watched in horror as he dropped to his knees next to the van and began sobbing into his hands. She was almost afraid to look as she inched closer. Without having to see, she knew Emily was dead. Max's pain was too intense for it to be anything else. She took another tentative step forward and was dismayed by what she saw over his shoulder.

Emily's body was a tangled mess. She'd been facing the backseat during the crash, and her neck had been broken as a result. Her face was a bloody mask, making it impossible to find the pretty girl she'd been before the accident. The right side of her body was crushed, bones tearing through fragile skin.

Max gathered her tattered frame in his arms and pulled her gently onto his lap, though she was far beyond feeling pain at this point. "Emily, Emily, Emily," he sobbed, rocking his dead wife.

Erika inched forward, wanting to offer him what little support she could, when lightning struck far too close for comfort, warning that they were in no way safe or out of the storm's danger zone. It lit the sky, illuminating Emily's ravaged body for a moment before pitching them back into the hazy gloom the storm created. Her words of comfort changed to a warning. "Max, we have to go."

The usually easygoing man spun on her with an enraged snarl. "I just lost my wife, you monster. Don't tell me what I have to do!"

Erika jumped back, startled by the open hostility. She pressed a hand to her lips, fighting back tears that threatened to spill over her eyelids. She wasn't trying to be cruel. She'd liked Emily a lot. She couldn't even imagine what this man was going through, but they were in danger. It wasn't safe to stay here. She didn't know how to convey that to him without seeming crass.

In the moment of silence that followed Max's outburst, lightning struck a power line roughly forty feet in front of them. Deadly sparks lit the night as one of the wires snapped loose of the support.

Erika heard the buzz and could feel the electrical current as it raised the hair on her arms. The live wire smacked loudly against the ground as it landed, sending more sparks into the air. "Max," she warned again. Though it seemed impossible, the wind picked up speed, tangling her hair and burning her eyes.

Lifting them to the sky, her heart plummeted at the cloud formation above. Frantically, she grabbed Max by his hurt shoulder, trying to shock him back to the present. She needed his thoughts away from his dead wife and on his own survival. "Max! That is a funnel cloud! Do you know what comes next? A tornado. We have to get out of here. Now!" Without waiting for a reply, she reached into one of the broken windows and fought to pull out her duffel bag.

Her words seemed to jar Max back into the present. With one last kiss to Emily's forehead, he let her go. The next instant, he was by Erika's side, helping her pull supplies from the vehicle. "What will we need?" He hollered to be heard over the roaring winds and crackling wire that curled ominously against the ground.

Erika tossed him a backpack full of bottled water and nonperishable foods. She followed that with a first aid kit. The rest had been in the large suitcase in the back, but they didn't have time to locate it. They would have to survive with what they had. "Just this!"

Her eyes flicked to the funnel cloud and widened in horror when she realized it was descending its way slowly to the ground. "Just run!" she screamed. Tossing the strap of the duffel bag over her head, she did as she'd instructed Max. She ran.

Both of them sprinted as fast as they could through the mud and debris. They were both aching and uncomfortable, but they gritted their teeth and pushed on. Pushing their bodies through limps and sore muscles, they ran toward what they hoped was safety.

12

Burlington, Vermont
Peyton Rivers

Peyton sat curled up on the couch with Melody and Zeke. The three of them were watching the storm, taking turns flinching at every stroke of lighting or boom of thunder. Glancing once again at the clock, she said, "Your dad will be home any minute." She'd been repeating this over and over again for nearly two hours.

Derek had said ten minutes. Something was wrong. She'd tried calling his cell phone seven times since then, and there was never any answer.

Peyton anxiously nibbled on her fingernails as she looked to the door, willing Derek Alison to suddenly be behind it. To her utter disbelief, as if in answer to her prayers, there was a sudden knock at the door. "Your dad's home!" she cried in relief, jumping to her feet.

"Why is he knocking?" Melody asked thoughtfully as she followed her babysitter to the front door.

"I don't know," Peyton replied. "Maybe he has his hands full with camera equipment. Maybe..." She swung the door open and trailed off in surprise. She gaped at the person on the front porch in stunned silence for a moment, unable to figure out why he was here. "Jamie?" she finally asked in confusion.

Shifting his weight uncomfortably from foot to foot on the Alisons' front porch was her boyfriend Jamie. The two of them had lived next door to each other since they'd been in diapers. They'd started out best friends, bravely facing kindergarten together as a united team. Then they'd shared their first kiss together under the monkey bars in fourth grade just to see what it was like. They'd officially become a couple in the seventh grade and had been spending every spare moment together since, seeing each other almost every single day.

Today shouldn't be one of those days. She wasn't the type to sneak her boyfriend over while she was babysitting. The two of them spent plenty of time alone together without needing to resort to this. Derek Alison would not be happy to see Jamie at his house.

"You shouldn't be here," she chastised in a hushed voice as if the absent Derek might hear and discover Jamie's presence. "I'm babysitting."

Jamie ran a hand through his shaggy blond hair and glanced anxiously over his shoulder before returning his gaze to her. "You have to come with me."

Peyton gave an embarrassed bark of laughter. "I can't do that." She leaned toward him and lowered her voice. "I'm a little busy at the moment. I can't just up and leave with you. We're having dinner together tomorrow night. Whatever this is, can't it wait until then?" Her brows furrowed as she studied him with uncertainty. "What has gotten into you?"

He opened his mouth to respond, but Melody cut him off as she peered around her babysitter to stare at the stranger on the front porch. "Who's that?" she asked, pointing at Jamie.

"This?" Peyton asked, shooting her boyfriend a warning glare. "This is Jamie. He's a friend of mine."

"Oh," Melody said, accepting the newcomer's presence easily. "Have you seen my dad?" she asked Jamie, tilting her head adorably to the side.

Jamie's intense gaze flicked down to the little girl who barely reached his knees. "No. No, I haven't, sweetie." His hazel eyes returned to Peyton, their depths swirling with urgency. "Bring her. We have to leave. Now."

Peyton wanted to argue, but faltered upon observing the expression on her boyfriend's face. He was afraid. "Jamie, what's wrong?" Distractedly, she reached her arm out and wrapped it around Melody's shoulders. "We can't leave. Mr. Alison will be home any minute. He told us not to leave the house."

"Forget what he said!" Jamie cried, nervously looking over his shoulder toward the side yard once again. "I think he would want you to leave."

Peyton blinked at him in shock. Jamie had never raised his voice to her before. Ever. He was always sweet, charming, and polite. "It's storming," she argued, stepping out onto the porch to wave a hand at the ugly clouds. "We..." She trailed off when her eyes caught sight of the tornado that was making its way toward them from less than a mile away.

It was still too far out for her to see particulars, but there was no mistaking the debris that was being tossed about. The trees were easily identifiable while they were being ripped from the ground and swept up into the funneling mass, but once there, it was impossible to discern them from any other objects. "Oh my God," she whispered in horror.

Jamie grabbed her elbow and pulled her toward the porch stairs. "That's why we have to go!" He grabbed Melody's hand and tugged the girl outside, his movements frantic. "The Killington family a few blocks over has a storm cellar next to their house. They're on vacation, but I'm sure they wouldn't mind us using it."

As Melody stumbled onto the porch after Jamie, her eyes followed theirs to the approaching twister. Her tiny mouth opened and she screamed, but the sound was drowned out by the roaring wind.

Deciding that Jamie was right about Derek permitting her to leave in such a situation, Peyton grabbed Melody and pulled her close. "We have to go," she explained to the little girl. "We're going to the Killingtons'. They have somewhere safe for us to stay."

Melody shook her head in terror. "I...I can't. I'm scared."

Jamie knelt down in front of her and began explaining in calm, reassuring tones how important it was for Melody to leave with them right away.

While her boyfriend tried to convince the child to come along willingly, Peyton leaned back into the house. "Zeke!" she screamed. "Zeke, come!"

The puppy inched its way toward her, whimpering. His hind quarters quivered in terror with every tentative step he took in her direction.

Peyton lunged forward and grabbed onto Zeke's collar. She didn't have time to be gentle or wait for him to come to her. Wrapping her fingers around the collar, Peyton pulled him onto the porch and slammed the door shut behind him. She kept a tight grip on his collar, keeping him pulled against her left leg. She spun to face Jamie and Melody, hoping her eyes weren't as wild and frightened as they felt.

The others didn't seem to notice. Jamie was busy with Melody, and the little girl's eyes were trained almost desperately on his.

Jamie was tugging playfully at one of Melody's braids in an attempt to distract her from their terrifying surroundings. "We'll be okay, kiddo. I promise that Peyton and I will get you there safe. Once we get to the storm cellar, you won't have to worry about this weather anymore. It is the safest place in the world." He gave her an encouraging smile. "I need you to be brave for me until we get there, okay? Can you do that?"

Melody bobbed her head. "I can be brave."

Jamie gave her an encouraging mock punch to the jaw. "Atta, girl," he said amidst her giggles. He stood up and gave Peyton a cursory evaluation. Seeing the panic in her eyes, he pulled her toward him and gave her a firm kiss. "You too. Bravery, Peyt."

She nodded jerkily. "Yeah. Brave. Okay."

He kissed her quickly on the forehead, grabbed Melody's hand, and took off into the storm. He moved as fast as he could in the direction of the Killingtons' house, urging Melody forward as he went.

Taking a deep breath, Peyton raced after them. She kept her hand wrapped tightly around Zeke's collar, keeping the dog close to her side. Moments after running out into the downpour, her clothing was drenched through. Her hair hung in wet clumps in her face, making it difficult to see more than a few feet ahead of her. She stumbled along, clutching the dog's collar as if it were a lifeline.

Thunder clapped loudly from nearby, the ground itself shaking with the force of it. Peyton jumped, and Melody gave a little cry of fear.

"We're okay," Jamie encouraged, curving his arm around Melody's shoulder as they ran. "You're doing great. Just keep going, sweetie. Don't look at anything else. Just keep running for the Killingtons'. We're almost there."

Peyton kept her eyes trained on Jamie and Melody, their retreating figures a guide in the nearly blinding rain. Her heart was beating so frantically and painfully in her chest as she raced after them that she feared it might explode. She ignored this as best as she could and pressed on.

She was so intent on keeping Jamie in her sight that she didn't notice the root sticking up from the ground until her foot got lodged into it. It hooked around her sneaker. Not realizing she was caught, Peyton only managed to get herself lodged tighter under the root when she attempted to take another step. She gave a cry of surprise as she was dragged suddenly to the ground.

Jamie turned back at the sound of her yelp and let out a curse. At the same moment, Zeke raced forward, being re-

12

leased by Peyton's fall. Jamie barely managed to grab onto the dog's collar as it bolted in his direction. He shoved him toward Melody before he even had a solid grip. "Take Zeke and run! Get to the Killingtons'. I'll help Peyton!" he hollered over the wind.

Melody nodded obediently and took off in the direction of their goal.

Peyton was yanking at the vines that were tangled around her ankle from underneath the exposed root when Jamie dropped to his knees in front of her.

"Thank God you were okay," he said with relief as he helped her pull at the vines, tearing them away. His hazel eyes lifted to hers only momentarily before he was giving her trapped foot his complete attention. "When I turned on the news, I almost had a heart attack I was so worried."

Peyton shook her leg free, her breathing labored as she tried to see through the drenched locks of hair that covered her face. "I can't believe you came for us." She glanced over her shoulder as the tornado advanced toward the Alisons' home, leaving a path of destruction in its wake. "We would have died if it wasn't for you."

Jamie gripped her elbows and helped her to her feet. "Like I could leave you," he teased reproachfully as he pulled her to him for a quick hug. "You're my girl."

Peyton closed her eyes for a moment, leaning her ear against his chest so she could faintly hear his steady heartbeat. *I love you*, she silently thought, but was too cowardly to tell him aloud.

Jamie pressed a few quick but affectionate kisses to the top of her head. "You have no idea how worried I was." He held her tightly for a moment before he moved to pull away. Just as he did, there was an earsplitting cracking that resounded through the night. "Peyton, get down!" Jamie screamed.

She barely had time to lift her head in fear before she was shoved roughly to the side. She hit the dirt painfully for the second time in as many minutes. Coughing on the rain water that had forced its way down her throat, she struggled to her knees.

"Jamie?" she hollered worriedly into the downpour. Forcing her hair out of her eyes, she searched frantically for her boyfriend. "Jamie?" she yelled, her voice edging on hysterical. Then she saw him.

The large tree in which she'd gotten her feet tangled in the roots had snapped at the base. The enormous maple had come crashing down where they'd stood only moments ago.

Jamie had shoved her out of the way, but hadn't been able to do as much for himself. He was trapped under the tree, the bulk of it resting across his chest.

When Peyton caught sight of him, looking so battered and helpless under the heavy mass, a terrified scream ripped from her throat. "Jamie!" Racing to his side, she dropped to her knees in front of him. "Oh, God. Jamie."

He coughed feebly, air trying to force its way through crushed lungs.

Peyton moved his head so it was in her lap. "Jamie," she cried tearfully. "It's okay. I'm going to get you help. You're going to be fine."

"No," he struggled to croak out. "I'm dying. Go to the little girl. Leave me."

She gave a gasp of horror at his suggestion. "No! How could you even say that? I'm not leaving you!"

Jamie reached out the hand that wasn't pinned down by the tree and grabbed weakly onto one of hers. "She needs you."

Tears began streaming down Peyton's cheeks, trekking a path through the dirt that covered them. Their salty taste mixed with the rain water that trailed into her mouth. "No," she sobbed. "Did you leave me in second grade when Billy Carter was picking on me in the hallways? No. I can't. I can't leave you."

"You...have to," Jamie groaned, ending his sentence with a cough.

Her tears doubled when she saw blood in the corner of his mouth, signifying that he was bleeding internally. "You're hurt bad, but—"

He cut her off. "Peyton, I love you."

She dipped her head over his, her tears dripping onto his face as his grip on her hand began to slacken. "Jamie, I—" It was too late though. She watched the light fade from his eyes, watched him die without any hope of stopping it.

Her heart constricted in agony as she realized she'd missed her opportunity. She should have said it. She'd had her chance a few minutes ago and she'd stayed silent. Now he was dead, and she'd never be able to tell him that she loved him.

With a wracking sob, she punched the tree pinning him, scraping her knuckles on the rough bark. "Damn it! Damn it, why? Why *him*? I needed him!" Still sobbing, she ran her fingers through his soft blond hair, trying to draw comfort from the familiar action.

With tears still streaming down her cheeks, she bent to press a gentle kiss to his forehead. "I love you, Jamie." When his eyes stared back at her, unresponsive and unseeing, she let out a scream of rage. She couldn't look at him like this. She refused to remember him like this, broken and lifeless.

Scrambling to her feet, she glared at the sky. "I needed him!" she screamed with all of her might. As if in response, the wind whipped louder, almost knocking her off her feet. She stumbled against it, moving robotically in the direction of the Killingtons' house.

As she saw it come into view, her chest heaved in anguish. They'd been so close. Just a few houses more. If only she hadn't tripped...

"Peyton!" Melody's little voice called out. "Peyton, hurry!" The little girl waved from the storm cellar doors. "It's too heavy! I can't get it open!"

As Peyton watched the little girl struggle with the heavy, wooden door, Jamie's words echoed in mind. *She needs you*. Steeling herself, she moved to the girl's side. "Let me help." Even she struggled with the dense door but managed to get Melody, Zeke, and herself safely inside.

Just as Peyton was about to shut the shelter door, Melody gasped and pointed in the direction they'd come from. "Look! My house!"

Peyton and Melody stood side by side and watched the tornado as it ripped through the Alisons' home.

"My SpongeBob bowling ball was in there," Melody said dejectedly, her young mind unable to fully comprehend the severity of what had just transpired.

"I'll buy you a new one." Eyes wide, Peyton edged the little girl down the steps into the protection of the cellar. Reaching above her head, she slid the bolts of the door into place, securing Melody and herself inside.

As soon as she was positive they were safe, she crumpled to the floor, unable to continue.

"Peyton, where is your friend?" Melody asked innocently, her big brown eyes full of concern.

That was enough to cause Peyton to break down again. She buried her face into her knees and cried. Her sobs came ragged and painful, her heart aching for the boy next door that she would never again see.

Melody tiptoed her way over and wrapped her tiny arms around her babysitter. "Peyton," she whispered, tucking her head against the older girl's. "He saved us. Your friend was a very nice boy. He's my hero."

Peyton reached a hand up to half hug Melody. "He's my hero too."

12

Silver Gate, Montana
Dr. Kyle Phelps

Kyle looked at the list of Silver Gate citizens in his hand and tried to ignore the roar of the volcano behind him. It wouldn't help to worry or panic. At this point, there really wasn't much he or Dave could do for anyone who hadn't evacuated the area. They were mostly here to be a comfort; Dave to show that the authority figures hadn't abandoned the town and Kyle to explain information only he knew.

"Looks like they've already split," Dave commented from beside him as he peered into the window of the homey log cabin of whose porch they stood on. He let out a wry chuckle. "I wanted them to ship that damn barking dog of theirs off for years. Turns out all I needed was the volcano to go *boom* to get my wish," he joked without much humor. His poor attempt at comedy was followed by a weary sigh. "How many houses does this make so far?"

"We've visited two hundred and thirty-four residences," Kyle read from his notes. "Two hundred and twelve were already abandoned, thirteen were in the process of packing up, and nine households are refusing to leave."

Dave nodded. Removing his hat, he wiped sweat from his forehead with the back of his hand. "Do you...do you think most of those people are going to make it out all right?"

Kyle grimaced in response. "We just have to hope that most people fled the area as soon as they heard the information Ryan fed the press. If they evacuated right away, they might have a fighting chance."

Dave motioned to look at the next name on the list, but gave another sigh and lowered his clipboard. "We're wasting our time, aren't we? Anyone we find isn't even going to have enough time to get out, are they?"

With only a slight hesitation, Kyle shook his head. "No. It's too late already." Wiping sweat from his own face, he lowered himself to sit on the porch steps.

"What about my Penny?" Dave asked, lowering himself to sit next to Kyle. "Is it too late for her?"

Kyle shrugged, sitting back with a weary sigh. "Who knows?" he answered honestly. Turning to look at Dave, he offered the only hope he could give. "Ryan's a good boy. I'm confident he'll do everything in his power to keep your niece safe."

Dave grunted, but didn't disagree.

They sat in silence as hot ash rained down, looking like a grotesque, gothic snow storm.

"Looks like it's going to be a white Christmas after all," Kyle commented with a sardonic smirk. "That weather man be damned."

Dave chuckled and went to comment when a loud noise to their left distracted him. The sound of snapping trees filled the air followed by the frantic shriek of birds.

Both men looked in the direction with expressions full of anxiety.

"It's the lava," Kyle said quietly. "It's getting close."

Dave had to swallow thickly before he was able to speak. "Then before it's too late, I'd like to thank you for staying behind and helping me try to get some of these people out. It was my responsibility, and I appreciate your sacrifice."

"Don't...mention...it," Kyle whispered in shock, his sentence fragmented and his words trembling as he caught his first glimpse of the lava.

It was flowing toward the two men, roaring its violence to the world. The weight of the heavy ash crushed trees as it fell, snapping branches with loud cracks. The river of lava seemed bent on destruction and death, pulling everything into its fiery grave. There was no escaping its brutal trajectory of destruction, and they were next in its path.

12

Nagoya, Japan
Nikki Stanton

As she stumbled along through the trashed streets of Nagoya, Nikki tried to keep her eyes from straying to anything other than the road in front of her. There were injured and dying people all around. She couldn't bear to look them in the eyes and still keep moving. It seemed inhumane. Yet, there wasn't anything she could do to help those people. They were going to die no matter what she did. Stopping would only guarantee her own death.

Riddled as she was with remorse and guilt, Nikki pressed on. Her shoulders were aching terribly from the weight Tony was putting on them, but she tried to ignore the pain. Fear and adrenaline kept her going. When...if she got a moment to relax, she was going to be very sore.

Noticing her obvious struggle, Scott called over in encouragement. "Almost there, guys. I think we're as close to the center of Japan as we're going to get. We're just outside of Gifu." He pointed a few blocks ahead. "See those buildings over there? We need to get inside one of those and get to the roof. We stand our best chance there. Those buildings are sturdy. They've survived the initial shock waves. They should be strong enough to withstand the water."

As if sensing it was being talked about, water came flowing toward them with a loud whoosh.

Nikki, Scott, and Tony heard screams from behind them and turned to see water rushing through the street in their direction. The water was only knee-high, but it was traveling fast.

"Brace yourselves," Scott warned, his tone wavering at the mere sight of the deadly water as it tore a path toward them, dragging down injured people.

The three of them stopped their forward progress to await the approaching tide of violence.

"Steady. Steady," Scott advised as the swell came closer and closer. "Here it comes. Hold on."

Though she set her stance shoulder width apart and prepared herself for impact, the water still swept Nikki from her feet. She hit the pavement and was submerged for a moment. She just had enough wits about her to see Tony falling as well out of the corner of her eye.

Scott was the only one who managed to stay on his feet, but just barely. He staggered against the pressure, fighting to stay upright.

When Nikki surfaced with a gasp a few feet away, he began sloshing his way toward her. "Nikki! Here!"

Looking frightened and disheveled, she struggled to her feet. She fought against debris as she started making her way slowly in his direction, her progress hindered by the rushing water. "Where's Tony?" she hollered over in concern.

"I don't know! He went under after you did!"

"I'm over here!" Tony's voice came from their right. He was clinging desperately to a lamp post, his hands clawing to maintain purchase on the slippery metal.

"We're coming," Scott called in reassurance. When he reached Nikki, he grasped her hand and squeezed her fingers in his own. He pulled her in against his side and pressed her hands to his shirt.

He didn't need to tell her what to do. Nikki gripped the fabric in her fists with a viselike hold, the skin around her knuckles turning white with her exertion. Together, they made their way through the treacherous waters over to Tony.

Without even needing to discuss it, they each automatically moved to opposite sides of their injured friend and looped his arms over their shoulders. Nikki moved in against Tony's left side, hugging the right side of her body to him while Scott mirrored her actions on the right side. She now had a tight grip on Tony's shirt instead of Scott's, but she clung to him all the same. Every time one of them went down, it felt as if the odds of getting back up diminished significantly. There was too much chaos and danger around for them to slip up.

"We have to keep moving," Scott encouraged as they began trekking toward their destination once again. "We're nearly there. Just keep pushing ahead."

During their unscheduled stop to get their friend, the water had only gotten higher. It now reached Nikki's waist, making progress difficult. Her legs were so heavy it felt as if she was wearing weights on each of them.

The current was pushing them toward their desired building, but its momentum was too much, causing them to battle to stay upright. They'd barely made it one block before she was gasping for each breath, struggling to draw oxygen into her abused lungs as she struggled to support Tony. She sucked in ragged gulps of air, sputtering on water that splashed up into her face due to her own movements.

She struggled under the weight of Tony's arm, and as the water reached chest level, she had the panicky fear of drowning. She couldn't keep the water out of her mouth, and she couldn't extend to her full height with Tony leaning so heavily on her.

The water was getting too deep. They'd never make it to their intended building before she was fully submerged. "Scott," she called out, wanting to tell him as much, but her words came out garbled as another rush of water hit them. It washed over her head from behind and splashed into her face.

He must have gotten the gist of what she was trying to say, because Scott stopped suddenly. "We're never going to make it on foot. We're going to have to swim for it." He set them with a piercing look as he huffed out his instructions. "The main floors are going to be flooded by the time we reach the buildings. We're approaching from the back, so climb up one of the fire escapes. I'd suggest the building with the news station logo on the outside," he said, pointing toward a tall, imposing building. "We'll get inside on a higher story and proceed to the roof from there."

He received two nods of agreement.

Nikki released her tight grip on Tony's waist. "It's a good plan. I can't keep this up much longer. I think swimming will be easier on all of us."

"Let's go," Scott urged. "Get to the building. I'll stay at the back of the group to make sure you both get there all right."

Without needing to be told twice, Nikki dove under the water and started toward their target with a practiced breast stroke. The current was easier to deal with now that she wasn't fighting to stay on her feet, and the water around her ears drowned out the sound of frightened screams. She had to be careful to avoid chunks of debris floating in the water, but it was easier to get around swimming than it was lugging Tony next to her.

She'd crossed half the distance to the building before she thought to look for her companions to make sure they were keeping up. When she couldn't locate either Scott or Tony, she whirled in the water, frantically searching for them as she tried to ignore the panic that began rising inside of her. When she finally found them, her heart dropped in concern. They were nearly back where she'd left them.

There seemed to be some kind of argument going on between the two of them, and Scott was yanking forcefully at Tony's shoulder, his face red with anger.

"Scott?" she called out anxiously. She was now able to tread water without her feet even brushing the ground. The water was only getting higher, and they weren't making any progress. As she slowly began paddling back in their direction, their heated words carried to her.

"Come on," Scott growled, yanking on Tony once again.

The other man opened his mouth to argue but then seemed to finally go docile. He allowed Scott to slide an arm across his chest from behind as a lifeguard would do to a struggling swimmer and pull him in Nikki's direction.

"He doesn't know how to swim," Scott informed her with irritation as the duo reached her side a few minutes later. He was forced to speak loudly to be heard over the roaring waves. "He was just going to let us leave him behind," he informed her, his voice laced with exasperation. "He said he would rather drown than inconvenience us any further."

She gasped in disbelief, her head sinking underneath the water as she momentarily forgot to tread. "Are you nuts?" she shrieked at their equipment manager the moment she surfaced.

"I've held you up enough," Tony said with frustration. "I don't want to be responsible for getting either of you killed. You should have left me behind."

"You would have died," she cried with horror. "You would have drowned!"

"Better than having one of you die trying to help me," he countered.

"We're a team," Scott grunted with the effort to swim and haul Tony along with him. "We stick together. You would never abandon one of us. We're sure as hell not giving up on you."

"Agreed," Nikki said firmly. She began swimming toward their intended building once again, but her progress was slow because she didn't want to get too far ahead of them. "We are going to make it out of here alive. Together. We're going to be the most celebrated news team America's ever seen once we get home," she informed them over her shoulder.

She pressed forward, breathless but motivated. She tried to look toward the future for added inspiration to keep going. "When we get off this cursed island, I am getting a pedicure and an hour massage."

There was a moment of silence, and then Tony said, "As soon as I get out of here, I'm going golfing. I haven't been golfing in years. I kept meaning to go, but never made the time to do so."

Scott chuckled before giving his input. "Well, after I get a shower and clean all this grime off of me, I'm booking a reservation at the most expensive restaurant there is back home, Shebelle's or whatever it's called."

"Steak," Tony said in approval of the extravagant restaurant's specialty. "You're going to fill your stomach with the best food money can buy."

"Not just food. I am buying the most expensive bottle of wine the place has to offer. Me and hopefully the most drop dead gorgeous reporter I've ever seen are going to get a little tipsy." A wolfish grin spread across his lips. "Then I'm hoping to take her back to my place and successfully seduce her."

"It'll work," Nikki tossed out in assurance. "I have a feeling she'd like that very much."

"Is that debris or are you suddenly sporting an erection?" Tony teased.

"Ha ha," Scott said dryly. "I could always let you sink."

"Sorry. Sorry," Tony apologized with a chuckle. "It's just weird seeing the two of you like this. I thought you'd be mooning over her while she stayed completely oblivious for all of eternity. I never expected you to finally man up and go for it."

Nikki turned in the water to laugh at them both when a forceful wave sent her careening into the building they'd been swimming for. The water thrust her against the side of the fire escape before she even had time to react. She'd been moments away from grabbing onto the metal handrail when the wave had sent her forcefully toward it. Her proximity caused her to smash into it with bone-jarring violence, eliciting a cry of pain from her lips.

Water rushed over her head, and she felt a tugging suction from the angry, whirling waters. It dragged her further under the water, pulling her down amidst debris. "Scott!" she screamed into the water as she was drawn even further down, the words rising in front of her in ominous bubbles.

She thrashed against the pull of the current, struggling with all of her might to claw to the surface. Her lungs were burning as she fought, making it harder for her to function. After what felt like an eternity, she somehow managed to break the surface with a desperate gasp.

As soon as she surfaced, she was smacked once again into the railing by the next wave. Her body hit with enough force to bruise. Survival instinct had her hands clawing at the slippery banister that separated her from the stairs. She clung to it as the water tried to once again yank her down into its lethal depths.

Nikki wrapped an arm around the handrail the moment there was a break between waves, giving her a better hold. The fire escape was made of a thick, sturdy metal meant to withstand nature's attacks. It had one horizontal handrail connected to many smaller vertical bars that kept a person safe from falling off, but it was now blocking her from accessing the stairs. She would need to climb over the handrail to get to safety. It was also these vertical bars that had abused her body so terribly. Lifting a foot out of the water, she wedged it between two of the vertical bars to give her more resistance against the water. Once she was certain of her grip, she wrenched her head around to look for her companions.

Scott was struggling to stay above water as well as keep Tony afloat. "Don't you let go of that railing," he hollered to her through gritted teeth. "Climb."

Obediently, Nikki began pulling herself out of the water. She wanted desperately to help them, but she could barely keep herself afloat. She would be more of a hindrance than anything else if she was to swim back out to them. It was best for her to get to safety so Scott didn't have to worry about her as well as Tony.

Adjusting her grip on the handrail to pull herself over, she gave a soft hiss at the pain the metal sent racing through her palms. She'd been gripping the banister of the fire escape so tightly it left welts on her skin. If she lived through this, she was going to have some serious blisters to deal with.

With a grunt of effort, she hauled herself over the handrail to the grated fire escape flooring next to the windows of the third story, her back hitting painfully against metal. The instant she hit the unforgiving steel, she rolled onto her stomach and looked down for Tony and Scott.

They were still a few feet away, struggling against the current as they approached. The force of the waves slapping against the building was pulling them in toward the fire escape much swifter than was safe. "Brace yourself," Scott warned. "This is going to hurt!"

Nikki held her breath as they collided with the metal railing. Scrambling to her feet, she leaned over it, searching the rough waters for them to resurface after being pulled under by the icy grip of the current.

The seconds seemed to drag by. A minute felt like five. Just when she was about to jump back into the water after them, they surfaced.

Scott sputtered and coughed. He barely managed to suck in a large lungful of air before he was sucked back down.

She watched them struggle against the waves, her heart in her throat. "Come on, Scott," she pleaded, though she knew he couldn't hear her. "Just grab onto the railing!"

Every time he even came close to the fire escape, he or Tony was pulled back under the water by the raging waves. They were slammed into the hard metal over and over again.

Nikki could see them weakening. A person could only suffer so much physical abuse before their body gave out. Neither one of them seemed to be making any progress. In fact, it seemed as if their time under the water was starting to exceed their time above it. "Don't give up," she begged frantically.

"Enough!" Tony shouted as he surfaced, gasping for air. Both of them were submerged for another moment after his outburst before they popped back into view. "We're either going to drown or be crushed against the side of the building," he wheezed breathlessly. He struggled feebly against Scott's grip. "Just let me go. Save yourself."

Scott tightened his hold on the other man, which caused his head to momentarily dip underwater. "I'm not going to just let you die!" he said stubbornly when his head broke the surface again. "We'll make it." No sooner were these words out of his mouth when they hit the wall of the building and were dragged underwater again.

Nikki's grip on the railing tightened and a yelp of fear escaped her lips. They couldn't keep this up much longer. Every time they disappeared from view, she feared it would be for the last time.

Just as alarming was the water that was beginning to seep through the metal grating of the floor at her feet. With a sound of frustration, she began moving up the stairs, trying to keep away from the rising flood. "Scott! Tony!" she screamed, leaning over the handrail.

"Here," came Scott's exhausted voice. "We're here."

"You need to let me go," Tony growled out. "You tried your hardest, for which I am extremely grateful, but I am not going to let you die in vain! This water is just too much for any one person to handle while towing someone else with them. We'll both end up drowning if you don't let me go."

"No one's going to die," Scott said obstinately.

"You can't hold me and climb onto the fire escape." He shot a weary look to the metal railing they were repeatedly being slammed against. "You're going to be crushed to death." Tony gave a bellow of frustration. "She needs you! For once in your life, be responsible. Take care of her. Survive. For her."

Nikki saw the briefest moment of hesitation cross Scott's face.

That one moment of uncertainty gave Tony the opening he needed. Pulling his fist back, he punched Scott in the jaw.

Instinctively, the other man released him.

As soon as Scott's grip on him loosened, Tony kicked away from his friend with all his might, sending himself shooting toward the road and away from his companions.

"Tony! No!" Nikki screamed in horror. She watched as the current yanked him in the opposite direction to the building across the street.

He hit one of the large windows and it shattered on impact. Tony was sucked through to the building's interior, yanked beyond their view. Water and debris raced in through the gaping cavity behind him in a violent swirl.

"No!" Nikki screamed uselessly. "Damn it, Tony! Damn it!" A strangled sob escaped her throat, and she punched a fist into the railing in front of her as she realized their friend was lost forever.

"Fuck," Scott snarled in frustration. "What the hell was he think—" His comment was cut abruptly short by a grunt of pain as he slammed up against the railing of the stairs a few

12

feet below Nikki.

With a groan of effort, he slung an arm over the rail and held on as tightly as he could as another wave slammed against his back. When the wave pulled away, the churning water nearly ripped him from the fire escape. The muscles in his arm bulged in protest as they were pushed to their limits. As soon as he had an opportunity, he began pulling himself up amidst the sound of his own grunts and moans.

As soon as she could reach him, Nikki grabbed the back of Scott's shirt and helped pull him over the handrail onto the relative safety of the steps.

The moment he was over the railing, Scott's muscles gave out. He collapsed, taking Nikki down with him. He knelt above her as he desperately tried to catch his breath, each inhale coming in sharp, painful-sounding gasps.

She watched as his expression changed from fatigue to guilt.

"I didn't want to let him go," he wheezed. "I tried. I tried to hold on. I swear I did."

Nikki nodded her head. "I know," she assured. From her position underneath him, she reached up and cupped his face in her hands. "You did everything you could."

Scott nodded, closing his eyes and taking a deep breath. He kept his face lowered, his expression one of anguish.

Watching his face in silence, Nikki felt the tears building in her eyes. Try as she might to fight it, a sob escaped her. Tony was dead. There was no way he could have survived being sucked through that window even if he *could* swim.

Scott's eyes opened at the sound of her soft sobs. "Hey," he whispered, his eyes softening at the sight of her grief. "Don't cry." His face was sympathetic as he said, "Tony wouldn't want us to give up hope. He sacrificed himself so we could keep going." He turned his head enough to kiss her palm. "We're okay. We're gonna keep going. We'll be fine."

She nodded tearfully. "I'm just so scared." She wiped tears and flood water from her cheek with the back of her hand. "I thought you were going to die. I thought you were going to leave me alone. I can't do this without you. You can't leave me."

From inches away, Scott stared into her eyes in silence, his expression saying all the words he couldn't yet articulate. His gaze was soft and caring. There was a look of complete affection on his face that complemented his determined protective streak.

When water began lapping at their legs a few moments later, it subconsciously drew his attention away from her. Reluctantly, he broke eye contact and climbed to his feet, helping Nikki to hers to keep them from lying in the filthy water. "I'm not going anywhere, sweetheart," he vowed quietly. "I promise you that."

Nikki gave a sob of relief and clung to his waist. She buried her face into his shoulder and drew strength from his solidness.

Scott ran his hand over her hair, comforting her for the short moment they could spare. Grudgingly, he was pulled back to the severity of their situation when water lapped at his knees, reminding him of their predicament. "We need to get moving," he whispered against the top of her head.

Before pulling away, she whimpered softly into his shoulder at the thought of having to continue. "Where to?"

Water pulled at the railing, causing it to shudder and shake. Their dangerous surroundings seemed to be answer enough.

"We have to get off of this fire escape," he instructed. Taking her hand, he led her up the few steps to the next landing, which was even with a window. He peered into what seemed to be an office. "Stand back," he advised, nudging her behind him.

Using his elbow, Scott smashed in the glass. It shattered, raining shards down onto an abandoned desk. Tucking his hand in the sleeve of his shirt, he knocked the larger pieces out of the way with his fist.

Once he had the more dangerous shards of glass removed from the frame, Scott helped Nikki step through the window and down onto the desk. He followed her through a moment later, his shoes crunching on the glass as he carefully stepped around pens, papers, and other office supplies to keep himself from slipping. He'd barely dropped to the carpet when water started dribbling in the window they'd just entered. "We better find the stairs before we get flooded."

Nikki nodded her agreement and took his hand. Lacing her fingers with his, she led him across the small office to the door that opened to the hallway. "The stairwell is at the end of the corridor. I can see the emergency lights."

The power was long gone, so they had to inch their way

slowly down the hall. Scott caught his foot on something lying in the middle of their path and nearly lost his balance.
With a soft curse, he righted himself.

Moving toward the wall on his left, he placed Nikki directly in front of him. His left hand released her to press flat
against the wall, and his right rested protectively on her
waist, guiding her forward.

"The light from your camera would be nice right now,"
she commented simply to keep herself from freaking out as
her feet sloshed through the now ankle deep water. Something brushed her leg and she shivered, not even wanting to
know what it was.

"I lost the camera," Scott admitted.

She gasped and spun to face him in her surprise. She
peered up at him in the near darkness, having to stand so
close that the front of their bodies brushed for her to be able
to see him at all. "You lost the camera?" she asked in shock.
"What happened?"

"When you..." He shook his head with a derisive snort. "I
freaked out when you got separated from us. I pocketed the
memory card and dropped the damn camera like it was on
fire." His hand still on her waist, he walked her backwards
the last few feet to the stairwell. "Lame, I know."

Nikki moved backwards into the soft lighting of the stairwell, relieved that they were no longer feeling their way blindly
in the dark. "You rushed through a panicked crowd to rescue
me. That isn't lame. It's romantic. You're my knight in shining
armor." She walked backwards up the first two steps before
she came to an abrupt stop, causing him to bump into her.

With a giggle, she lowered her head over his with her
added height and kissed him. Her lips move softly along his
as her hands lifted to cup his cheeks in her palms.

Scott groaned softly, his own hands sliding up to caress
her hips.

She smiled against his lips, reveling in the newness of
their mutual feelings for one another. "We've only got a million steps until we reach the roof. Think you can keep up, old
man?" With a girly laugh, she turned and sprinted up the
staircase.

San Fernando Valley, California
Clara Dichello

Clara sighed heavily and looked down into her cosmopolitan while trying desperately to keep her boredom from being too obvious. She was attending an awards ceremony, was even nominated for two awards of her own, but she was finding it all very tedious. Shake hands and socialize, don't forget to smile, and most importantly, be sure to show cleavage.

She hated functions like these. The only men who got into these events were rich old perverts or creeps. If a man was so desperate to rub elbows with porn stars, he wasn't the type of man to bring home to mommy. Though, being a porn star, she supposed she wasn't the type most men would want to bring home to their own mothers, so who was she to complain?

"Don't look so down," a voice whispered with a giggle in her ear. "There's free booze."

Clara turned with a smile to face her best friend Leah. "This party is lame," she whispered back.

"Lame?" Leah asked in disbelief as she tossed long black hair over her shoulder. "Honey, I just got offered twenty grand to sleep with some hoity-toity businessman. Tonight is business gold."

"We're porn stars, not prostitutes," she responded lightly before taking a sip of her drink. She and Leah might be best friends, but they had different perspectives about their jobs.

Leah was all about the money. She would do anyone or anything if it meant making a few extra bucks.

Clara was the opposite. She wasn't in her line of work for the money. She did what she did because she enjoyed it. She took pleasure in having sex with good-looking men. She was very selective in her partners, and she was extremely careful when it came to STDs.

No, she did not have daddy issues like the thoughtless stereotype suggested she would. She'd been adopted at a young age by a wealthy couple whom she adored. She'd had a wonderful life in which she'd kept her very active sex life private.

It wasn't until after her parents passed that she considered doing her hobby professionally. They'd left her a large sum of money, not to mention their mansion, so it had never been about the money. She just loved sex and got a thrill out of being watched. She'd earned the title of the Porn Princess due to her wealth. Because of this, many men were clamoring to work with her, but she kept the list short.

Not insulted by Clara's comment, Leah just laughed. "Tomato, tomato," she countered, using the classic conflicting pronunciations of the word. "All I know is that is a hell of a lot of money."

She took a sip from her wine glass and surveyed the room. In a sing-song voice, she said, "I think I know someone who wouldn't mind throwing some extra money your way." Leah nodded at a man across the lavish banquet hall. "Mr. Price has had his eye on you all evening."

Clara looked in the direction her friend nodded and grimaced.

Benjamin Price was standing in the far corner, his eyes glued to her. His eyes were always glued to her, and it freaked her out. Most men who stared usually ended up offering her a proposition. Not Benjamin, though. He never made any offers. He just watched her silently from across the room. A few times, he'd engaged her in odd conversations. How were her finances? Was she happy with her life? What type of hobbies did she have, despite the obvious?

His questions unnerved her. It was like he saw himself as a knight in shining armor who planned to rescue her from her troubled life. Only problem was, she didn't need rescuing. She liked her life how it was.

"No thank you," she said jadedly to Leah. "Mr. Price makes me uncomfortable."

"Would you like me to threaten him for you?" a third voice offered.

Clara spun with a brilliant smile to face Bruce Allemande, a fellow "actor" and close friend of hers.

From the moment she'd met Bruce, she'd hit it off with him. He was fun and zany. They both had the same taste in food and movies. They both had a love of bungee jumping. Most importantly, they both had the same taste in sex. They'd filmed quite a few movies together, both walking away pleased with the experience and footage.

Besides working together so well, they were close

friends. In fact, Bruce was the closest thing to a boyfriend she'd had in years. They got together on weekends to curl up on his couch and watch movies. They went out to dinner. They made love in front of his fireplace. There was no exaggerated grunting and moaning when they were alone together. It was sweet and tender. It was real. Clara had to guiltily admit she had warm and fuzzy feelings for Bruce.

At this thought, she smiled at him with fondness and shook her head. "No. Don't threaten him. He's harmless."

Bruce slung an arm over her shoulder. "Whatever you say, beautiful." Leaning in, he gave her a quick kiss. On her arched eyebrows, a lazy grin spread across his lips. "Just making him jealous," he explained with a teasing smile.

"You always look for excuses to kiss her," Leah said with a roll of her eyes. Tossing her hair once again, she changed the topic. "How's your evening going, Bruce? Any business opportunities for you?"

"If you're asking if I'm whoring myself out, the answer is no." He shared a quick smile with Clara. Like her, he was more selective with his partners. "I am up for a leading male award, though. That's a bright spot in my night. It's for a film I did with a certain beautiful redhead." He elbowed Clara. "If I win, the producer says he's planning on filming a sequel. You in?"

Clara perked up for the first time all evening. "I'd definitely be willing to do a sequel. Is this the one with—" She broke off with a little noise of surprise as the ground suddenly shifted under her feet. "Oh!" she cried in alarm as the walls began to vibrate and the alcohol in the small glass in her hand quivered.

"Earthquake," Leah said calmly as things stopped shaking. "Damn California."

"I was just thinking that I am not *that* tipsy yet," Bruce said with a light laugh. "Give it a few hours and I'll really feel like the walls are moving."

For as long as she'd been living in California and as many minor tremors as she'd experienced, they still made Clara nervous. "I hate those things," she said with a little shiver as she checked to make sure her dress was still wrinkle-free.

Bruce wrapped a comforting arm around her shoulder. "Don't you worry—" He broke off in surprise as the floor began trembling once again. He lost his balance and stumbled back into one of the waiters.

The tray of drinks in the man's hand tipped, crashing to the ground. The glasses shattered when they hit the floor, leaving a hazardous trail of shards.

Bruce shot the waiter an apologetic grimace. Putting a hand to both of his female companion's backs, Bruce ushered Clara and Leah from the center of the room. "We should get to a doorway."

Instead of letting up like usual, the vibrations in the floor only seemed to grow more violent. People began to get nervous, giving anxious cries of alarm as dust and plaster began shaking loose from the ceiling.

"Wow," Leah chattered, her voice vibrating with the effects of the quake. "This is a bad one. I—" She broke off with a shout as part of the banquet floor gave way. The sound of cracking wood could be heard amidst the suddenly genuine alarm that rose up from the occupants of the building. The wooden floor in the center of the room split, revealing a gaping crater beneath it that led to the basement. The new fissure in the flooring caused the rest of it to tilt downwards toward the hole.

Clara cried out as she tumbled to the ground. Far beyond feeling embarrassed by her fear, she lowered herself to her stomach to balance herself on the unsteady ground. She looked over her shoulder at the banquet hall to see that the center of the floor had split further, dividing the room nearly in two. With a sharp gasp of fear, she dug her nails into the floor in an attempt to find some stability. She then lowered her cheek to the floor to help herself feel grounded. The tilt to the ground wasn't drastic, but it was alarming.

"Are you all right?" Bruce's voice asked from beside her.

Clara turned her other cheek to the floor to gaze over at him. "I...I'm okay. Just a little shaken up."

He was kneeling next to her, his face pale and hands shaking. "We need to get outside while the tremors are stopped. If they start up again, we could be in some serious trouble. The whole building could collapse into the basement."

It wasn't until he mentioned it that Clara even noticed the tremors had stopped. The chasm in the floor had become more frightening than the earthquake that started the whole mess. She nodded her head emphatically in agreement. "Yes. Let's get out of here."

Before they could even think about moving, frantic shouts rose up from others in the room. "Leonard fell through the floor when it collapsed!"

"So did Tyanna," a second voice called out.

"They're trapped down there!" the first voice yelled. "I can't even see around all the rubble. Someone call nine-one-one!"

Bruce's hand was suddenly on Clara's hip, urging her upward. "We have to get out of here," he murmured in her ear. "We can call nine-one-one once we get safely outside."

Clara nodded and climbed cautiously to her hands and knees. "Leah," she said breathlessly to her friend, "we need to get to the door."

From the other side of Bruce, Leah gave a disgusted snort. "You're just going to leave? There are people trapped down there! You two should be ashamed of yourselves."

"We can't be of any help in here." Clara tried reasoning with her friend. "We'd be assisting the injured people better by getting outside and calling for help. We could show the rescue workers where to go."

"You're just being a coward," Leah spat.

"Leah," Bruce said pleadingly. "We can get help. At the very least, they're going to need rope to get to Leonard and Tyanna. A hundred people standing around aren't going to be of any help."

"Leah, please," Clara added beseechingly to her friend. "You know he's right."

Climbing unsteadily to her feet, Leah stumbled in the direction of the gaping hole. "You two go. I have to stay here. I can't leave them." As she took another step toward the hole, a loud cracking sound filled the air.

People screamed and dove out of the way as a section of ceiling came hurtling to the ground. It hit the already broken flooring and pulled more down with it as it crashed to the basement.

With a gasp of surprise, Leah staggered as the ground shifted beneath her feet from the force of the impact. Her left heel came down dangerously close to the edge of the widened chasm.

"Leah!" Clara screamed. "Be careful!"

"Get back over here!" Bruce hollered with demand in his tone.

As if the current devastation wasn't enough, the ground began to tremble again. The whole room rocked and vibrated, tearing at the suddenly unstable structure.

"Leah!" Clara screamed as more of the ceiling came raining down around them. She gave a yelp of alarm as a chunk of plaster fell dangerously close to her own head. She ducked her face into her arms to keep herself from inhaling the dust that filled the air. When she looked up again, she watched in horror as another large section gave way, rebar and plaster showering down onto Leah.

A piece of rebar pierced through Leah's shoulder as the debris knocked her to the ground. It pinned her to the floor as more rubble piled on top, weighing the petite woman down.

Clara watched helplessly as Leah struggled to push the debris off of her, but it was too much, too heavy. She wanted to go to her friend, but Bruce held her back, his arm wrapped tightly around her waist to keep her from getting to her feet. She knew there wasn't anything she could do until the room stopped spinning, but Leah looked so alone, so frightened.

Leah tried once again to push some of the debris away. A chunk of plaster she tossed to the side hit the rebar that skewered her shoulder, jarring it. She gave a sharp cry of pain and instinctively jerked in response. This only ended up hurting her more. With a wail of agony, she lowered herself back to the floor. She then went still, the fight leaving her as she realized she'd never be able to get loose on her own. "I can't do it by myself," she whimpered. "Someone help me!"

When no one came rushing immediately to her aid, her head turned in Clara's direction. "Clara," she pleaded weakly. "Clara, don't leave me." The ground shifted again, drawing a gasp of agony from her throat. Blood began seeping through the white fabric of her cocktail dress, making a dark stain on the once pristine garment. "I'm so scared."

A sound of horror escaped Clara. She pushed away Bruce's protective grip and struggled to her knees. Slowly, she inched in Leah's direction. Once closer, she could see the damage to her friend's shoulder. The rusted metal tore through flesh and muscle, leaving a grotesque wound that caused her stomach to turn. "Leah," she breathed in horror as she continued to inch closer. "Oh God."

"God doesn't love us," Leah said weakly. "We're porn stars."

Reaching her hand out to grasp her friend's, Clara whimpered with a sob, "That's not true."

Swallowing past her pain, Leah asked, "Then why would he let this happen?"

Before Clara could answer, she was suddenly grabbed from behind. She was thrown backwards, landing roughly on her backside as a desk came sailing down from one of the floors above.

Bruce landed on top of her with a grunt of exertion forcing its way through his lungs. His knees and elbows hit the ground brutally, drawing a sound of pain from him.

Over his shoulder, Clara could see the desk as it fell through the open space left behind by collapsed floors, picking up speed as it went. While she watched, the desk came crashing down onto Leah's skull, crushing it upon impact. The weight of the desk pulled down more of the flooring, leaving less and less space for survivors. Leah's body fell to the basement level, disappearing from sight.

It all happened in an instant. Clara didn't have time to even process what had happened before the floor suddenly gave way beneath her.

Bruce's arms came up to cover her head, protecting her as best as he could while the two of them plummeted to the basement as well.

A grunt of pain escaped her as the section of flooring they were on hit the basement concrete with a bone-jarring thud. She wasn't braced well enough, which caused the back of her head to hit the hard wood of the flooring beneath her with a crack. Stars danced before her eyes as pain raced through her ribs at the one story fall, and she had to blink a few times to clear her vision.

"Are you okay?" Bruce asked into her ear, his breathing harsh, his tone pained.

Slowly, she lifted her eyes to him to see that his shirt was torn and his shoulder was bleeding.

"You're hurt," she murmured in concern, still feeling half-dazed.

His hand reached out to gently touch her forehead. "So are you." When he pulled away, his fingers came back crimson with blood. With a sigh, he wiped it onto his ruined shirt and sat back on his heels to look up at the floor above. "We have to get out of here and soon. This whole building is

12

about to come down around us."

Biting her lip, Clara first surveyed their surroundings. Parts of collapsed ceiling lay everywhere, blocking them off from reaching the stairway that might take them safely back upstairs. They were boxed in with no way to go but up, the way they'd come. Her eyes then followed his gaze to the chasm above. "What are we going to do?" she asked. There was no way anyone would have stayed behind after that last round of tremors. It was suicide. Getting back onto the ground floor was going to rest on their shoulders.

A face appeared unexpectedly in the hole, contradicting her thoughts. "You're going to climb out," Benjamin Price said firmly.

"Benjamin," Clara gasped in surprise. His face was one of the last she expected to see right now. "Y...you're still here? I figured whoever was left would have split by now." A quick glance around had proven there was no one alive in the basement besides herself and Bruce. Even before their fall, people had been filing for the exits. It seemed unlikely that there would have been anyone left to notice their absence.

Benjamin rolled his eyes. "Yeah. I guess I'm dumb." He appeared to be lying on his stomach above them, leaning over the hole in the floor. A chunk of ceiling crashed to the ground too close to his head for comfort and he cringed. "Find things to stack until you can reach my hands. I'll pull you up." He grimaced. "I'd hurry. This place isn't going to be standing in a few minutes."

Clara blinked in shock for a moment before turning to Bruce.

He shrugged and then turned to look around them. After a quick perusal of the basement, he pointed to a large toolbox that stood at least three feet high. "There. Help me push that underneath the hole."

It looked heavy, and she was in heels, but Clara followed Bruce. She peered down at the red, metallic box, nodding slowly. "This looks like it might do," she agreed.

Together, the two of them struggled with the weight of the box, scraping it loudly against the cement flooring. A few times, they got caught up on debris, forcing them to lift the box and carry it.

The muscles in Clara's arms trembled under the weight, and she lost her grip once, almost crushing her toes. It only took a few minutes, but it felt more like an hour to get the box positioned underneath the spot where Benjamin lay.

"Hurry," Benjamin urged, waving a hand toward Clara. "Climb up. I should be able to reach you."

Clara was staring up at Benjamin with uncertainty when Bruce grabbed her around the waist. He pulled her toward him and gave her a firm kiss. "Go ahead. Get up there. I'll be right behind you." He lowered his mouth over hers for a second, more lingering kiss.

Clara slid her arms around his neck and returned the kiss, but her eyes peeked in Benjamin's direction. She noted that he averted his eyes while Bruce kissed her, looking extremely uncomfortable.

When Bruce released her, Clara stepped back with a roll of her eyes in annoyance at Benjamin's behavior. Why did the person helping them have to be a starstruck fan with a crush? It was unnerving. She should be worrying about staying alive, not about finding herself in the midst of a love triangle. With a huff, she began scaling the large toolbox, cringing when she smacked her knee against the protruding knob of a drawer.

Bruce's hands were suddenly on her hips, helping her climb. He held her steady as she scaled the awkward metal structure, using drawers as footholds to her climb.

As she slowly ascended to the top of the box, she felt Bruce's hands run possessively over her backside and couldn't help but smile. He was letting Benjamin know that she was already involved in a relationship...if that's what you wanted to call it.

The show wasn't lost on Benjamin. His face was pinched in annoyance as he held his hands out to her. "Quickly! Take my hands."

Clara hesitated only a second before reaching up and grabbing his forearms. She'd just gotten a good grip when a chunk of ceiling from two floors above came crashing down toward them.

"Move!" Bruce yelled in warning.

Simultaneously, she and Benjamin broke apart.

Clara tumbled backwards off the tool box. She gasped in fear as she momentarily fell through empty space, but was quickly relieved as she felt Bruce's waiting arms catch her, keeping her from hitting the cement flooring.

Benjamin rolled out of the way as the chunk of plaster hit the ground where his shoulders had been only moments ago. "Shit," he cursed loudly from above.

She watched with wide eyes as the debris slammed into the box directly where she'd been standing only moments before. A large cloud of dust followed the wreckage, and she coughed roughly as it forced its way into her lungs before she could protect herself.

"Come on," Benjamin hollered through the murky air. "Now! The building is coming down."

Before she could move, Clara was hauled to her feet.

Bruce shoved her back onto the box, urging her toward Benjamin. "Go! Go!"

Lunging, she latched onto Benjamin's forearms, gripping them as tightly as she possibly could.

With a grunt of effort, he began hauling her upward.

Their progress was slow, the debris falling around them a constant hazard. Clara's feet scrabbled at the air as Benjamin pulled at her, trying to dodge clutter as it fell around him.

She tried to keep her terror under control, but her heart was hammering a constant drumbeat against her chest cavity. Her nails dug into Benjamin's wrists, and she made a mental note to apologize later...if she lived through this nightmare.

Loud noises filled Clara's ears that she couldn't even fathom. It sounded like the entire earth was screaming in anguish. She couldn't imagine how the building was still standing at all with the horrendous sounds that caused her ears to ring and her stomach to instinctively clench in terror.

"Get her out of here!" Bruce hollered over the noise. He scrambled up the tool box behind her. His hands were suddenly on her backside as he shoved her upward toward Benjamin.

She gave a cry of surprise as she flew suddenly through the hole due to Bruce's added boost. A large chunk of concrete went sailing past her head, missing her by inches. She heard it hit the tool box with a loud clanging bang that shook the already rickety foundation of the building.

As she came sailing unexpectedly into him, Benjamin fell backwards.

Clara landed on top of him, the air rushing out of her lungs. She waved toward the hole where Bruce was still trapped, trying silently to convey her concern for him. She fought to breathe, a wheezing sound escaping her lips as she struggled. "Get up!" Benjamin yelled. "Run! Get up, now!"

Clara was still disoriented when he yanked her to her feet. Instead of running for the exit as instructed, she whirled back toward the gaping hole in the floor. "Bruce!" She staggered as if drunk, her legs fighting her every step.

Benjamin grabbed her upper arm, wrapping his hand easily around its entirety. "Let's go!" he demanded, his voice a deep growl.

When he tried to yank her toward the exit, Clara wrenched her arm away. "Are you insane?" she shrieked. "Bruce is still down there! We have to help him."

He once again grabbed her arm, tugging her forcefully toward the door. "The building is collapsing in on itself. We are going to die here if we don't leave now!"

Clara struggled against him, alarm filling her at the tight grip he had on her arm. "I am not leaving Bruce behind!" Her heels dug into the floor as she tried to stop him from dragging her across the floor against her will.

"He's dead, Clara!" Benjamin yelled in frustration. "And if we don't move, we're going to be dead too."

"No!" Refusing to believe him, Clara kicked the toe of a stiletto high-heel aggressively into his shin.

Instinctively, Benjamin released her.

The moment he did, she raced to the hole and dropped to her knees at its edge. She peered into the destruction below, searching frantically for her lover. When her eyes finally found him trapped under a pile of rubble, a strangled sob forced its way out of her throat. "Bruce!"

Benjamin had been wrong. Bruce wasn't dead. He was trapped, his once virile body crushed under the weight of debris. Blood was trailing out of the corner of his mouth, and his eyes looked vacantly up at her. "Clara," he struggled to say, his voice an abrasive croak. "Run."

"Bruce!" She was leaning forward in an attempt to see him better when Benjamin grabbed her around the waist and hauled her backwards away from the hole. As he forced her toward the exit, another section of flooring came crashing down, falling onto the already mounting pile covering Bruce.

Clara struggled and kicked against Benjamin, trying to break free of his grasp, but he was too strong.

He overpowered her, yanking her roughly toward the front door. Shoving her in front of him, he forced her ahead as he moved.

As she resisted him at the doorway to the outside, Clara could see that the exposed support beams of the building were giving their final stand. They swayed and trembled, threatening to collapse. Despite the danger, her resolve didn't waver. "We have to go back for him! We have to—" Her words were cut short as one after another the beams burst, exploding in a shower of concrete as they gave way to the forces of nature and the fallen debris that weighed unevenly on them. Entire sections of the building began to cave in, obliterating anything unfortunate enough to still be inside.

Benjamin stumbled in the doorway that would lead them safely outside, his movements unsteady as he fought the elements and the woman in front of him. With a growl of frustration, he shoved her out the entranceway as the building came down behind them.

She hit the cement of the parking lot, scraping her hands as she fell. As she rolled to lie on her back, Clara's eyes widened in horror at the sight. The rest of the building collapsed in on itself just as Benjamin had predicted, crushing any remaining occupants. Concrete caved in, sending up a cloud of dust. The collapse of the structure was so forceful that it shook the very ground beneath her. "Bruce!"

She clambered to her knees to stare at the trashed remains. At some point, the earthquake had ceased, so she was able to kneel steadily enough on her own, but her entire body trembled with shock. "Oh no," she sobbed desperately. "No. No."

Benjamin's hands were suddenly on her shoulders. "Clara, I'm sorry."

She whirled on him, eyes burning with fury. "Don't tell me you're sorry!" she screamed through tears. "You wanted this! You've been stalking me for months just looking for an opening." She broke down into hysterical sobs. "Bruce. Oh God, Bruce." Her hands ran over her face, smearing her carefully applied makeup. "You wanted him out of the way," she sobbed pitifully.

Benjamin sat back on his heels, his expression stung. "You really think that?" He paused, running his hands over his face. "It doesn't even matter," he mumbled to himself.

Lowering his hands, he set Clara with a serious look. "Listen, I don't know how closely you've been paying attention to the news, but the end of the world is going on out there. Things are really bad. Everywhere. I have a bunker I've been preparing. I think we should—"

Clara jerked away from him. "I'm not going anywhere with you, you creepy fuck. What I want is to find a nice police officer and inform him that you just forced me to watch my fucking boyfriend die!" She knew she was being spiteful because of the dramatic events of the day, but she couldn't help but add her next nasty comment. "I want to file a restraining order."

Benjamin stared at her for a moment in silence before sighing. "All right," he said evenly. "Let's go." His wary expression gave away that he was about to royally piss her off. Stepping forward, he hefted her up to sling her over his shoulder. He held tightly to the backs of her thighs, letting her head hang down toward his back.

Her crying came to an abrupt halt at this turn of events. Her tone was now filled with rage as she screamed, "Get your hands off me, you pervert! This is kidnapping!" Her voice was shrill and piercing. She felt Benjamin cringe, and her lips curved with a malicious smirk.

"I will never have sex with you," she informed him nastily. "You are a sick, demented pervert. I don't care how long you keep me locked in your mother's basement, I will never touch you! Ever!" Curling her hand into a fist, she punched his back. "You can go fuck yourself!"

Benjamin suddenly whipped her down, setting her on her platform heels.

Clara shot him a smug smile and shoved her red curls out of her eyes. "You're giving up then? So you're a coward along with being a pervert?" She saw his jaw clench. Because she was hurting over the loss of Bruce, she wanted Benjamin to hurt as well. "I wouldn't have sex with you if you were the last man alive. You disgust me," she spat.

With a growl of agitation, Benjamin grabbed her by the shoulders and forced her to look him in the eyes. "Clara, I'm your brother."

CHAPTER 6

Cody, Wyoming
Ryan Williams

Ryan put a hand to his face and rubbed wearily at his tired eyes. They'd been on the road for nearly four hours. On a normal trip, it wouldn't have even taken two hours to get to Cody. Now, roads were littered with debris and other vehicles trying to make their way to safety.

He and Penny were merely lucky to be alive at this point. Ash was falling in thick clumps, leaving a dense layer on the roads. It looked like every child's dream snow day only the snow was black and choking.

They'd been driving southeast as fast as Ryan's pickup truck could take them. Worry for Jacob plagued his thoughts. His little brother was trapped in Denver, barely out of the blast zone. He only prayed Jacob was safe, hidden away from the nightmares consuming the globe.

"Ryan, he's okay." Penny's soothing voice broke into his thoughts.

He gave a derisive chuckle and glanced at her out of the corner of his eye. "Am I that transparent?"

"You were always transparent to me," she said with a soft chuckle. "That's why I liked you so much."

He grimaced, but then shot her a playful grin. "So it was pretty obvious that I wanted to get into your pants almost the first day I met you?"

"Why do you think I let you so soon?" Her cheeks flushed pink at memories long past. "You were special. Others had to wait a lot longer than you, Mr. Williams. A *lot* longer."

"Well, I appreciated it. You were my first real girlfriend. You were pretty damn important to me, and the fact that you were so good with Jacob made me love you even more."

"You loved me?" Penny asked, bolting upright in her seat in astonishment.

"Don't sound so surprised. Sure, I loved you. You were

my world." He let out a longing sigh. "Ah, to go back to those days when life was simple. I miss lounging in bed with you on Saturday mornings, watching cartoons and eating pancakes covered in strawberries and sugar."

"I miss your pancakes," Penny murmured. She closed her eyes and pictured the fluffy goodness in her mouth. When her eyes reopened, she gazed at him thoughtfully. "Why did you never tell me you loved me?"

He shrugged one shoulder, his eyes trained on the road. "I was young, barely out of high school. It was new to me. I wasn't used to feeling, let alone vocalizing such things." He paused before adding, "You never said it either, you know."

Penny leaned her cheek against the headrest and stared at him. "You were the first decent guy I'd ever dated. I was afraid I'd scare you off."

They sat in silence for a moment, Ryan maneuvering the treacherous road while Penny gazed at him. He finally broke the silence. "Well, seeing as we're probably about to die really soon, it's safe to tell you that I loved you."

Penny tucked her feet up under herself, a small smile touching her lips. "I loved you, too."

Ryan gave a soft growl of annoyance. "A lot of good it does us now."

"Even though it's after the fact, it's nice knowing," Penny offered. "I feel that even if we die here, at least we know there was one moment in our lives where we were truly happy and loved. It makes this all so much less depressing."

Ryan veered around a large fallen branch that jutted into the road before glancing over at her, wondering how they could have messed up something so great. He tapped his palm against one of her thighs. "You should sit properly in your seat, sweetheart. I'm a good driver, but these roads are dangerous."

It was amazing to him how easy it was to fall back into calling her an old nickname. Things with Penny had always been easy, at least things between *them* had been. It was others who tore them apart, not a lack of affection. He watched her straighten out in her seat and sighed. "We really messed things up, didn't we?"

Penny shook her head, a frown on her pouting pink lips. "No. *We* didn't mess up. *I* messed up. I let my uncle come between us. I think he was afraid we were moving too fast, and he worried that because you had no one to take care of you, you might get into trouble. I think he was also leery about the fact that we were alone together when I was at your place with no parental unit to keep us from..." She blushed and looked down at her hands, which sat fiddling with the hem of her skirt. "He was trying to protect my innocence."

Ryan snorted in amusement and glanced at her with a crooked grin. "He was right on that account."

Her blush darkened, but a fond grin crept up her lips. "Yeah. He was right in that case. Only he never knew how sweet you were," she offered. "All he saw was a horny teen-ager."

Ryan shrugged. "I didn't help. I was constantly pushing his buttons, on purpose might I add. Don't be too hard on Dave. He was only trying to protect you."

"Mmm-hmm," she mumbled noncommittally. "I suppose there's nothing to be done about it now. The past is the past." Her eyes suddenly misted over at the thought of her uncle. "I've been trying not to think about it, but he's proba-bly dead already." Her voice wavered, and she bit her lip to hold back her tears.

Ryan reached out and took hold of her hand. "I'm sorry, Penny." He was surprised to find that he meant it. He and Dave hadn't gotten along in the past, but they both cared a great deal about the blonde sitting next to him. He wished there had been time to patch things up with the police offi-cer. "I'm just glad you're here with me now. You're right. The past is the past. Right now is all that matters."

Penny offered him a brave smile and squeezed his fin-gers. "You're right. It is."

Ryan returned her grin before looking back to the road. Because of the heavy congestion, he'd turned off the main highways and was using small back roads he found on the map in his glove compartment. They were making better time without other people in their way, but the debris was worse. He'd already had to get out of the car twice to move fallen tree branches out of their path.

The ash was so thick, so heavy that it was pulling trees down with its bulk. The ash was ankle deep last time he'd gotten out of the car and still falling heavily. He was starting to lose tread on the tires. If it got to the point where they had to walk, they were more than likely screwed. Denver was still very far away. The only saving grace was that rain had started to fall. It was turning the ash into slush, but it prevented it from getting any deeper.

As he was busy fretting over what their chances of survival were, a dog ran in front of his truck. Cursing, he veered out of pure instinct.

Their vehicle careened off the road and into the ditch that ran alongside the left of it. The driver's side slammed into the bank of a muddy hill. Contact with the hill had the truck coming to an abrupt halt, jarring its occupants.

Penny screamed, her hands flying to the dashboard as they rocked to a stop. "Oh my goodness," she gasped in surprise. "Are you okay?"

Trying to ignore the frantic pounding of his heart, Ryan calmly assessed himself for damage. His left shoulder was sore from where it slammed against the door, but other than that, he seemed fine. "I'm okay. You?"

"Fine," she assured. "Just shaken up a bit."

"Good," Ryan said thickly. "Sorry about that."

She nodded, giving a soft noise of forgiveness. "It's okay. It was the stupid dog's fault, not yours. Just get us out of here."

With a nod of his own, Ryan put his foot to the gas pedal. He wasn't totally surprised, but he felt his heart sink as the tires spun in the mud of the embankment, refusing to take them back onto the road. "Shit," he hissed. "This is bad."

Though she must have already known the answer, Penny asked, "We're stuck?"

Grinding his teeth, Ryan replied, "Looks like."

"So now what?"

He had to look away from her big, frightened eyes. Now he'd get the truck free or they were dead. "I guess I get out and push," he finally said, trying to keep his anxiousness from showing. He motioned for her to get out of the car. "I can't get out my door. I'm pressed up against the hill. Let me out so I can push. I'll need you to hit the gas when I'm ready."

Penny's head bobbed in obedience. "Yes. Of course. I can do that." She hopped out of the passenger side door and stepped out of the way so he could follow her.

Ryan hopped down and was about to make his way around the back of the vehicle when she placed a palm against his chest.

12

"Be careful, Ryan. I couldn't bear for something to happen to you after I'd just found you again."

He hesitated. Then, taking a chance, he wrapped his arm around her waist and kissed her. "I'm not going to waste my second chance."

Penny touched two fingertips to her lips with a delighted smile. "Good to know," she said, voice soft as silk.

He gave her a lingering look. Then he headed around the back of the truck to check out the tires.

The ditch was small, but it was quickly filling with rain water running off the hillside. It was making loose, squelchy mud in its wake.

Ryan slapped a hand against the tailgate to get her attention. "Hit the gas slowly," he instructed. "I'm going to try to push us out." Bracing his feet, he pressed his hands to the back of the truck and waited for the tires to start moving. As soon as they did, he pushed with all of his might. He rocked the truck with his shoulder, trying to get enough traction for it to plow forward.

The tires continued to spin, kicking up mud and soggy ash to cover Ryan's trousers. A horrible whirring noise filled his ears as the tires struggled against the mud. Rain water dripped into his eyes, making it hard for him to see as he wrestled against the back of the truck in an attempt to send it forward onto the road.

When his shoulder began screaming in pain, he knew he couldn't take any more without causing himself serious injury. Backing up a few steps, he hollered, "Stop! Give me a minute!"

Penny released the gas pedal and glanced anxiously at him in the rearview mirror.

"Shit," he cursed, kicking at the slippery slope. If he didn't get them out of here soon, they were both going to die, buried by the ash that would continue to fall. As cruel as it might seem, he realized he should have just hit the dog and kept driving. Swerving to miss a dog that was already doomed to a fiery fate may have cost them their lives.

He gripped the spikes of his short blond hair and pulled with a frustrated growl. That was all he allowed himself, because it wasn't helping them. Lifting his eyes to meet Penny's gaze in the mirror, he hollered, "Let's give it another try."

Taking a deep breath, he prepared himself. If he wasn't

able to do this, they were dead. He had to keep pushing no matter what the damage to himself. Whatever minor damage done now was better than being burned alive by volcanic lava.

When Penny hit the gas, he gave a battle cry and shoved. He felt his left shoulder pop and gave a grunt of pain. It didn't feel broken or dislocated, just abused. Pushing the pain down, he continued to shove at the truck, digging his heels into the ground as best he could with the muddy conditions.

The truck suddenly lurched forward. It skidded as if on a patch of ice, then managed to get all four wheels safely back onto the road, rewarding Ryan for his efforts.

As soon as the truck was securely on the pavement, Penny screeched to a halt and threw it into park. She clambered out of the driver's seat, looking humorous in her tiny skirt and spiked heels. "We did it!" she cried joyfully. She raced to his side and threw her arms around him for a squeezing hug.

He returned the embrace for a moment. Then he kissed her forehead before pulling away. "Small victory," he said regretfully. "We need to get back on the road pronto."

She nodded in agreement and shuffled forward, heels clicking as she went.

Ryan moved to follow, but just as he took a step forward, a large boulder tumbled down the hill. He turned his head in its direction but didn't have time to get out of its path. The boulder caught him in the leg as it rolled, taking him down underneath it in the shallow ditch. The resistance of his body brought the massive stone to a halt, trapping him underneath its weight.

He let out a strangled cry of surprise before calling out for help. "Penny!" Before she could get to him, he was already shoving at the boulder, testing its weight.

Penny kicked her heels off and raced to him. "Ryan!" Dropping to her knees next to him, she frantically assessed the damage. "Oh, God. How bad is it?"

He cringed and tried to shift his position. The rest of his body moved, but his left leg was firmly immobilized against the ground. "My leg is pinned," he needlessly informed her.

Her expression pinched in concern. "I'm going to try to move it, okay?"

He knew it was the best option for the situation, but he didn't like it. Reluctantly, he nodded. "Do what you have to."

12

She placed the palms of her hands on the boulder and took a deep breath. "This is probably going to hurt," she warned.

Clenching his jaw, Ryan nodded.

"On three, okay?" She took a second deep breath and situated herself. "One...two..." She paused, flicking her gaze to his. Her gaze quickly returned to the boulder. "Three."

Though he was prepared for her action, it brought excruciating pain. He was unable to hold back his holler of agony as the stone ground his ankle into the earth.

"I'm sorry! I'm sorry!" Penny cried, her voice catching in her throat with emotion.

"Just get it off," he growled between gritted teeth.

Penny lowered her shoulder and went to double her efforts when a heavy wash of rain water came flowing down the hill. It was like being under a waterfall, only much less sanitary.

Penny gasped and gave a cry of alarm when the force of the water swept her from her feet and carried her a short distance away from Ryan.

He had bigger problems. The boulder was holding him down, keeping him trapped under the flow of water. He struggled to breathe around it, concern filling him as the water level continued to rise inside the ditch.

"Ryan!"

Penny's frantic, warbled voice reached him from around the rainwater that ran down the sides of his head. He felt her hands frantically grabbing at him.

She tugged and pulled, moving the part of his body not pinned down until he was out of the flow of water. Unfortunately, at this angle, he was forced to recline, the water lapping at his shoulders and only rising as the seconds passed.

As he watched the water levels steadily rise, he took a moment for himself, inhaling a deep breath of cool, night air. Then his gaze shifted to the blonde at his side. "Penny," he said, trying to keep his voice as calm and even as possible, "I need you to move that boulder right now."

She nodded frantically, looking on the verge of tears. "Okay. Okay." Positioning herself at his pinned knee, Penny grunted as she shoved at the heavy stone.

Ryan watched her arm muscles strain and her face turn red with exertion. Though she looked ready to collapse from the effort, the boulder barely even shifted.

Finally, she sat back with a sob. "I can't do it," she cried tearfully. "I can't do it."

"It's okay," Ryan said, his heart filling with defeat. "It's okay, honey."

Her tears came harder as she seemed to realize the hopelessness of their situation. "What are we going to do?"

He took a deep breath and closed his eyes, trying to build up the courage needed for his next statement. When he opened them, he was filled with resolve. "You're going to get into that truck and leave."

She blinked in confusion, not following him yet. "What?"

"I need you to take my truck and get out of here. I'm as good as dead, Penny. There's no need for you to die too."

"What?" she repeated. This time, her voice wasn't filled with confusion. It was filled with horror. "I'm not leaving you."

"In—" He broke off when the water that now lapping at his neck sloshed into his face. He shook the dirty water away before trying again. "The water is rising. In less than ten minutes, I am going to drown. I don't want you to have to see that. Please, Penny. Take the truck and go. All I ask is that you find Jake and tell him what happened to me. He needs to be told in person. He needs someone to mourn with, if just for a short while."

"Ryan, no," she sobbed desperately. "I can't leave you." She shifted on the ground, mud clinging to her stocking-covered knees. "I'll try again. It will move this time."

She positioned herself at his side to attempt another shove at the boulder, but he covered her hand with his. "No." He squeezed her fingers comfortingly. "You're only hurting me. We both know you aren't going to be able to move it. The sooner you accept that, the greater chance you have at survival."

"No," she cried wildly. "I'm not leaving without you. I can't."

He hated to yell at her, hated to be harsh, but he knew he had to. In order to save her life, he had to be firm. "Just go already! Get the hell out of here!"

As the full severity of their situation sunk in, Penny sat back on her heels, her expression stunned as utter hopelessness caused the color to drain from her face.

Nagoya, Japan
Nikki Stanton

Nikki lay in the big, lavish bed of the penthouse suite. She and Scott had gotten all the way to the roof, but he'd suggested they come back in after a while. It was impossible to stand out there and listen to the suffering going on below without starting to feel a little bit insane.

They'd curled up in the bed of someone who was more than likely dead, and Scott held her while she cried. She'd thought her sobs would never come to an end, but finally, they stilled.

Once she'd cried herself out, Scott made love to her. He'd been sweet and gentle. It was unlike anything she'd ever experienced before. It meant so much more than the shallow trysts they'd had in the past. It had been life altering for her...only a little too late in the game.

After their intimate encounter, they'd gotten dressed and curled back up on the bed to await the inevitable. Nikki was cocooned now in Scott's arms while they silently dealt with the gravity of their situation in their own ways.

Over the past half hour, they'd begun to hear the sound of water as it washed its way steadily up the stairs toward the apartment they resided in. In the past few minutes, it had started sloshing against the bedroom door.

"We should probably get back out on the roof," Scott murmured in her ear. He tightened his arms around her, trying to give her the last bit of comfort he could.

"The water's threatening," she whispered. "Our time is almost up."

"We can make it through this," he reassured, but Nikki could hear the doubt in his voice. "China will send ships to look for survivors. They aren't that far away. They wouldn't condemn an entire nation."

"They're probably having trouble of their own," she argued. "With Japan sinking, it's going to cause flooding for them. What if they can't afford to send help?" she asked in a wavering voice.

"They will." He kissed the top of her head before sliding out of bed. Turning back to face her, he held out a hand.

"Whatever happens, we'll be together. We're a team."

She took his hand and let him pull her to her feet. "We're a team," she agreed. Steeling her nerves for the sights that would greet them outside, she followed Scott to the small emergency door that led to the roof.

They were in one of the tallest buildings in the area. When the two of them made it to the rooftop, they were greeted by nothing but miles and miles of water. Occasionally, the remnants of another building's roof could be seen, but none of them held survivors.

"We can't be the only people left alive in Japan," Nikki breathed with overwhelming horror. "All those people..."

"There are others," Scott assured with grim determination. "There has to be. Surely the government got people out to safety." As he spoke, their building gave a sudden, loud groan and trembled.

Nikki cried out in terror and clenched his shirt tightly in her fist. "I'm not ready to die." They were mere feet away from being submerged and sinking fast. She heard the sound of windows shattering from the pressure of so many tons of water and knew it was the windows of the room they'd recently vacated. She nearly cried out for help, but there was no one left to listen, no one to hear her call.

"We can stay alive on the water for days," Scott said in an attempt to be encouraging as they lost more and more building to the raging waters. "This isn't the end."

She eyed the violently swirling currents and knew survival was an unlikely outcome. Even if they didn't drown, help would probably not be coming. She gave a pitiful sob and clung to her beloved cameraman. "This isn't the end," she agreed, if only to make him feel better.

A torrent of water came rushing over the lip of the roof, and it took her every ounce of control to keep from whimpering like a child. "Here it comes," she practically shrieked. "Here it comes. Here it comes." Though the water was only ankle deep, it had enough force to nearly knock her over as it swept over her feet.

Scott grabbed her arm and held her upright. "You can't fall down! You have to stay up!"

She didn't have the breath to respond to him, but she followed his advice. Locking her knees, she braced against the water as it swiftly rose against her calves. The water was just

12

breeching her kneecaps when she heard something that gave her hope for the first time in hours. "Scott!" She screamed over the roar of the water. "It's a helicopter!"

His head lifted as he searched the air for signs of proof. "Are...are you sure it isn't just the water you're hearing?"

As water lapped at her waist, Nikki strained her ears. She held on to this last bit of hope as her eyes searched the horizon. Finally, she saw what she was looking for. "There!" Off in the distance, a speck of black could be seen in the sky. "It's a helicopter! Scott, we're saved!"

He grabbed her waist and pulled her closer to him. "Come here." Bending his knees, he hoisted her up in an attempt to make them more visible.

Nikki waved her arms over her head, screaming to get the pilot's attention. "He sees us," she cried in delight as the helicopter angled in their direction.

The water was now lapping at Scott's chest, rising steadily. "I wish they'd hurry up," he grumbled, straining against the force of the rushing water while trying to keep her out of it as best he could.

She continued to wave as the helicopter approached, letting out peals of disbelieving laughter. "We're going to be saved." Grabbing his face, she gave him a spontaneous kiss. "You were right, Scott. This isn't the end." They were both exhausted and drained, but soon they would be dry and safe. They would be rescued where so many unfortunate people hadn't been.

She smiled down at him for a second before returning her attention to the helicopter as it angled slowly toward them, its propellers sending a stream of forceful air into their faces.

When it was hovering a few feet above them, the side door slid open. A Chinese man appeared an instant later. He leaned out and shook a hand desperately at Nikki.

She didn't speak Chinese, but the universal signal for *grab on* was easily understood. She stretched as far as her body would allow, fingers reaching for those that were just out of her grasp.

With a grunt, Scott hoisted her up higher. "Take his hand!"

The man continued to yell and wave his hand toward her. The way he leaned from the helicopter was dangerous, but he extended out over open air even further in an attempt to reach her.

The water was now covering Scott's neck, sloshing into his face as he struggled to breathe. With a final boost of energy, he gave a holler of effort and shoved Nikki upward. He threw her into the air, forcing her toward the man's waiting hand.

She was airborne for a second before the stranger's hand wrapped around her wrist. His other hand gripped tightly to a handle on the helicopter's wall to keep himself from being yanked out.

Nikki's feet dangled over deadly waters and certain death. She stared up at the middle-aged man with fear in her eyes. "Don't drop me," she begged. Her voice was barely a whisper because she was unable to speak over her terror. If he let go, she was dead. The water would carry her away and she would drown. "Don't let go," she sobbed.

A girl around Nikki's age suddenly appeared at the man's side. She reached down and gripped Nikki's forearm. "Don't worry," she assured in stilted English. "We've got you."

Though they were lifting her inch by slow inch, Nikki didn't feel secure until she sensed the safety of the floor solidly beneath her.

"You're safe," the girl told Nikki, easing her to lie back.

Nikki's relief only lasted a moment when she heard the sound of the helicopter's door sliding closed. "What are you doing?" she asked frantically. "Where's Scott?" The look that shot between the two strangers had her struggling to sit upright, desperate to see that her...boyfriend had been pulled safely aboard as well. Instead, she saw the helicopter begin to angle away from the building as it lifted higher into the air. "No!" she screamed. "Scott! You have to go back!"

The girl put a comforting hand on her shoulder, her dark eyes full of sorrow. "He is gone."

"Gone?" Nikki screeched as she shoved the girl's hand away so she could scramble toward the door. "He was right there! He was with me!"

"He jumped up so you could reach my father's hand. He did it to get you safely to us. He knew the water would take him once his feet were no longer planted. He did it for you." The girl ran a hand over Nikki's hair, brushing it back. "I'm so sorry."

"He can't be dead," Nikki sobbed, now clinging to the other girl. "He can't be dead." Iciness came over her that the chilly December waters hadn't been able to create. Scott was

12

dead. He'd sacrificed himself to ensure her safety.

Her sobs grew louder, more desperate. Overcome with grief, she dropped her face into her hands and let loose a wail of misery and despair. Her life may not have ended, but a large part of it was gone, a part she would never be able to replace. This day, her heart had suffered wounds she would never be able to heal.

Denver, Colorado
Jacob Williams

Jacob had spent the better part of the last few hours pacing. His hotel room was small and cramped, leaving no room for his six-foot-plus frame to stalk about. Worry for his brother had him almost manic. He couldn't think around it. Instead of doing something productive, like keep himself updated on world news, he paced about like a caged animal. He should have heard from Ryan by now. The silence of his phone made him fear something had gone wrong. He'd tried calling a few times, but on the rare occasions he was able to get through, there hadn't been an answer. "Where are you, Ryan?" He growled in frustration as his fist shot out and slammed into the wall.

As if in answer to his question, there was a knock on his hotel room door. He spun toward it with a look of amazed shock. Crossing the room in three quick strides of his long legs, he threw the door open. The strawberry blonde in the hallway caused him to emit a groan of disappointment.

Molly, the check-in girl, blinked at him for a moment in awkward silence. Then she said, "I shouldn't be here. You..." She shook her head and gave a derisive snort. "You weren't serious about that offer, were you?"

Jacob felt instantly guilty. "Yes," he quickly assured. "I was serious about my offer for you to come hang out here. I just..." It was his turn to shake his head. "I was hoping you were someone else is all."

"Your brother," she supplied, no longer feeling insulted.

He bobbed his head, trying to keep the concern from his expression. "Yeah. He said he was going to meet me here, but I haven't heard from him in a few hours."

"You're worried." Leaning against the doorframe, Molly stared up at him with big green eyes. "I was worried too..." She trailed off, her breath hitching with her next sentence. "I'm not worried anymore."

"You're not?"

She shook her head, lips pursed. "Nope. I was waiting for my parents to come pick me up because I was too afraid to drive out of here on my own." Interrupting her own story, she added, "Good thing too, because a tornado blew through the parking lot and swept away all those angry hotel guests." She grimaced. "I watched the check-out girl and her car get vacuumed up into the funnel then spit back out in the parking lot. Her car looked like an accordion." She shivered. "Anyway…next door neighbor called. My parents' house was apparently obliterated by some sort of sun flare while they were still inside. There goes my ride."

Jacob's eyebrows rose in surprise. "You seem calm about that." Meanwhile, he was trying to stay composed at the news of the tornado. He'd noticed the dark and ominous weather, but hadn't realized a tornado had accompanied it. He'd luckily been on the opposite side of the building and too caught up with his worry for Ryan. What he'd thought had been merely a bad storm turned out to be a natural disaster.

Molly shrugged one slim shoulder at his comment. "I am. What can I do about it really?" Despite her claims, the instant the comment was out of her mouth, tears began welling in her eyes. "I mean," she said with a little sniffle, "crying isn't going to help anything."

He didn't know the girl standing in his doorway, but Jacob moved forward and pulled her into a hug. He didn't have to know her to see that she was hurting and terrified. "Hey," he soothed as a loud, wracking sob escaped her, "you're safe here with me." He wanted to offer her other comforts, but there wasn't much he could say. Her parents were dead. That was a tough blow.

Molly didn't seem to need anything else but his company, because she clung to him as she cried. It didn't seem to bother her either that they'd only met this afternoon. Circumstances had thrown them together, and there was no sense being shy about it. "We're the only people left," she sobbed with fear. "They're dead. All of them, dead."

Jacob gently pulled her back so he could look into her jaded eyes. "This is a big airport, Molly. What you saw was the hotel's parking lot. That doesn't mean everyone in the entire airport is dead." He refused to believe that. It was impossible. "Others will come looking for a place to stay. This hotel is a beacon for survivors still inside the building."

Nodding, Molly lifted a hand to run the back of it against her eyes. Black mascara streaked her cheek. "You're right," she said, giving one last hiccupping sob. "There must be others, deeper inside the building. They'll come here once they realize how bad things are outside."

Jacob offered her an encouraging smile as he reached out to wipe away the mascara with his thumb. "All we have to do is wait."

She stared into his eyes for a long moment before inhaling a deep breath. "You must think I'm insane," she said, pushing past him into the room. "*I* think I'm insane. I show up at a strange man's hotel room and start weeping like a baby. Apparently, I'm not one of those take-charge personalities in a crisis."

"You witnessed a friend die and found out your parents are dead," Jacob offered as he closed the door and subconsciously locked it. "No one would be at their best after that. Cut yourself some slack."

Molly turned to face him. Shaking her hands as a means to expel stress, she took another deep breath. "I suppose. It's just that...I'm studying to be a nurse, right? I saw all that blood and I..." She trailed off with a grimace. "I puked in the lobby. I should have been able to handle this better. I'm *trained* to handle it better."

Jacob couldn't stop the laugh that escaped him. "The world is coming to an end, and you're worried because you threw up in the hotel lobby?" He crossed to the small dining set that dominated the main foyer of the room and flopped down into a chair. "Somehow, I don't think you have to worry about the hotel docking your pay."

Molly shook her head, a chuckle bursting up from her throat. "No. I guess you're right."

"Of course I'm right." He patted the chair next to him. "Why don't you sit down? Relax. The two of us can talk and get to know each other. We can hopefully make a nice distraction from—"

"Oh my God!" Molly cut him off.

Jacob sat up straighter in his chair. "What? I didn't mean anything by that. I just meant in a friendly—"

She interrupted him again. "I wasn't talking about you." She waved a hand dismissively in his direction. "I was talking about the plane!" Bypassing the offered chair, she rushed to the window and smacked her hands excitedly up against the glass. "There's a plane!"

Jacob was out of his seat in an instant and at her side. He

pressed his hands to the window frame on each side as he stood behind her, his breath catching in his throat. "What are they doing?"

"Escaping."

"To where?" he asked. "From what I heard, stuff is happening all over the globe. Where could they possibly think to go that isn't affected?"

"I don't know," Molly admitted. "It is all over." She shrugged carelessly. "You have no idea how bad the airport is. This room is on the far side of the hotel. From the lobby, I could see walls that collapsed. I heard an explosion somewhere inside the building. Wherever these people are going, it can't be worse than here. They're escaping."

He couldn't argue with that. Instead, he watched breathlessly as the plane started down the runway. All around the plane, balls of fire fell from the sky. They smashed into the ground, leaving craters in their wake. "They're going to get hit," he burst out anxiously. Another ball of fire came crashing to the pavement mere inches from the plane, causing him to flinch. "Those things are hitting too close. They'll never make it."

"They have to," she said desperately. "I can't take watching more people die. They just have to make it."

Jacob's hands gripped the wooden frame of the window so tightly that his knuckles strained in protest. "Come on," he coaxed. "Get into the air. Come on. Come on."

In front of him, Molly's shoulders were tense. "Please. Please," she begged. "Make it. Please."

When the plane's nose lifted into the air, they both inhaled sharply with hopeful anticipation. She spun to him and wrapped her arms around his waist in an impromptu hug. "They did it! They just might make it out of here."

He returned the hug with a laugh. "Wherever they're going, I hope it's better than here." No sooner were the words out of his mouth when a flaming ball hit the plane's left wing.

Smoke rose instantly from the spot, and the plane dipped dangerously to one side.

Jacob felt his heart drop to his toes. "Level out!" he demanded. "Level out!" He could see flames rising from the injured wing and knew instantly that they wouldn't be getting far. "They have to land," he said frantically. "There could be fuel tanks near the fire. They have to—"

A loud boom filled the air as the plane exploded. The force of it rocked the entire hotel, making the walls tremble and vibrate.

He grabbed Molly and pulled her face in against his chest, blocking her from the view but also from the dust that rained down around them from the ceiling. He turned his own face away and took a cautionary step back when chunks of debris began pinging against the window. He didn't want to look too closely at any of those bits for fear they might be human.

The hotel trembled again as the remains of the plane hit the runway with a screech of metal against concrete.

Jacob ducked his head against the top of Molly's, his shoulders flinching at the screaming sound of bending, burning metal. His breath was coming in short gasps that he struggled to control.

Molly clung to him as her shoulders shook with distraught sobs. "Everyone's dead," she wailed. "We're all that's left." Mournfully, she repeated, "Everyone is dead." Her face pressed into his shirt as her tears soaked into the fabric.

As he held her tightly for her comfort as well as his own, Jacob started to wonder if she was right.

12

Cairo, Egypt
Lilly Singh

Lilly had been quiet for the past ten minutes, caught up in her own thoughts. When she'd left her hotel room, the newscasts had only been getting more and more worrisome. Almost every station was running footage from an American reporter and her crew trapped in Japan as the country sank into the Pacific Ocean.

The reporter was a pretty little thing, not much older than Lilly herself. Her creamy complexion looked worse with each passing clip of footage until by the last piece shown, it was ghostly pale and clammy. Her eyes were wild, her expression terrified. There hadn't been any updates from the reporter or her crew in over two hours, and it seemed everyone was assuming the worst.

Lilly felt as if she could truly sympathize with the girl. She herself was trapped in a foreign country during this global meltdown. With appreciation, she turned to look at Christian as he maneuvered his rented truck through the desert. At least she had him. She wasn't alone. Though if they were to break down now in the middle of the desert, she would die with or without company.

A few miles back, they'd been forced to abandon anything that even resembled a road. A second earthquake had occurred shortly after they'd left the hotel. There were power lines down and debris everywhere.

The main roads had become impossible to navigate. They'd decided to take their chances with the open space of the desert. Christian had a navigation system he claimed would see them safely to the Khufu pyramid. She prayed he was right.

"Thank you again," she finally said, her voice sounding loud after the long silence. "I probably wouldn't have survived the night if it wasn't for you."

"I'm just glad you took me seriously," he said with apparent relief. "I sounded insane to myself. I can't imagine how I must have come off to you."

"A little crazy," she admitted with a laugh.

"Not nearly as crazy as that time Bethany Douglas blew

up half the chemistry lab though, right?" he asked with a laugh of his own.

"No! Not that crazy!" Lilly gave a delighted laugh. "She went insane! She was running around in circles screaming like a maniac."

Christian's deep laugh filled the vehicle. "Priceless."

Together, they both cried, "My butt's on fire! My butt's on fire!" Both of them broke into hysterical laughter despite the gravity of their situation.

"That was too funny," Christian said, taking a deep breath to refill his lungs.

At his comment, something suddenly occurred to Lilly, causing her laughter to abruptly cut off. She turned to stare at him with wide eyes, her breath held.

Noticing her sudden silence, he glanced in her direction. "What? What is it?"

"You..." Her brows furrowed. "You told me we'd never met before that time in front of the pyramid. Obviously, that isn't true. You've been lying to me." Reaching for her seatbelt, she couldn't hold back the sudden wave of panic that burned its way along her chest. "Stop the car."

He shot her a second look, this one full of apprehension. "Lilly, wait," he said cautiously. "I can explain."

His hesitation was like an admission of guilt. Lilly whipped her seatbelt off and pressed herself against the door. "I said stop the car!"

"Lilly!"

"Stop. The. Car!"

Christian finally slowed to a stop and threw the truck into park. "Will you just listen to me?"

As soon as she was able, Lilly threw the door open and scrambled out of the car onto the sand that had been serving as their road. The desert was blazing hot during the day, but now at dusk, it was starting to get chilly. She ignored the cold and marched forward, her tiny bit of remaining logic screaming at her that she would soon be lost in the desert during an apocalypse.

"Lilly, wait!" Christian yelled. He'd jumped out of the car as well, his feet hitting the sand with a thud. "You're acting crazy!"

She whirled to face him, her expression full of anger. "*I'm* crazy? You're the one who's been sneaking around like some deranged stalker, lying about *everything*."

"Lilly, the—" Christian broke off, unable to finish his sentence as the world began vibrating.

Lilly held her arms out in an attempt to keep herself balanced as the ground beneath her feet trembled. "Tex, what's happening?" she cried, though she already knew. It was another earthquake. This one felt even more powerful than the one that had ravaged Cairo earlier that morning.

"Just stay where you are," Christian advised. "It's just another tremor. It will be over soon."

She bobbed her head in agreement, knowing her eyes must be wide with fright.

"We're out in the desert," he called out encouragingly. "There's nothing around for miles that can hurt us." As soon as the words were out of his mouth, the ground split open underneath one of the back tires of his truck.

"Tex, look out!" she screamed as the tire sunk into the hole created by the quake.

He backed away from the vehicle with a look of astonishment on his face. "Holy..." As the crack widened, his eyes lit with horror. "The navigation system!" Even as the crevice widened and their truck sunk even deeper, he wrenched open the driver's side door.

"Stop!" Lilly yelled, inching closer in fear. "What are you doing? Get away from the truck! It's too dangerous!"

"Without a way to guide us to the pyramids, we'll die out here under the sun," he explained frantically. He climbed into the truck with a derisive snort. "We escape the end of the world only to die from dehydration out in the middle of the desert? I don't think so."

Seeing his point, she didn't argue. "Just be careful!" she hollered, her teeth chattering from the force of the earth moving beneath her feet.

Christian was inside the vehicle less than half a minute when the chasm opened wider. The passenger side of the truck fell with alarming swiftness only to get caught on the wall of the new canyon.

"Tex!" she screamed in terror as he disappeared from sight. Throwing caution to the wind, she raced in his direction. She was halfway there when the ground suddenly stopped vibrating. The sudden cease of movement caused her to overbalance. She went sprawling to the sand with a breathless gasp as the air was forced from her lungs.

She took only a moment to look at the spot where the vehicle had disappeared from before she was on her feet again and running. She skidded to a stop at the top of the fissure where the truck hung in a perilous position. It had fallen fully into the crevice a few feet below ground level and was lodged against the dirt walls. The passenger window faced the pit below with the driver's side, whose window was completely shattered, lifted toward the sky.

Christian was lying with his back against the passenger window with a stunned expression on his face. The window under his back had a spider web of cracks that made it appear as if it might shatter at any moment.

Below him, through the window, she could see a ravine that appeared to be bottomless. If the window gave out underneath him and he fell through, Christian was dead. "I'm going to get you out of there," she promised. "Just give me your hand."

Christian cautiously got up on one knee and waved off her hand. "I think I can climb the seats. I can get out of here myself if I'm careful." He shifted his weight ever so slightly so he could grab onto the end of the seat above him. That slight shift caused the glass under his knee to give way.

Lilly cried out in alarm as his right knee sunk through the now busted passenger window.

He gave a grunt of pain, and his fingers turned white from the tight grip he had on the passenger seat above him. "Okay. That sucked," he grumbled.

While she anxiously watched, he pulled his knee up and braced it against the glove compartment. The truck gave a soft groan, and he froze. His gaze lowered to the deadly chasm below. "I've got to be very careful," he said through gritted teeth, more to himself than to her.

"Be careful," she advised from above not a moment later.

"Really?" His head shot up and he gave her a crooked grin. "Thanks, Mom. I would have been totally careless otherwise."

"Shut up," Lilly said with a laugh, rolling her eyes. "Just hurry up, okay? You're making me nervous."

He gave a salute with his free hand and then began slowly climbing up the seat. Once he had his knee securely on the passenger side headrest, he began fumbling in the middle console. "Thank goodness," he breathed. "I was worried this was tossed out when the truck fell." He reached up and held out a map, a compass, and a handheld GPS system. "Here. Take these."

Careful not to upset the balance of the truck, Lilly knelt down and carefully took the items from him. She placed them next to her on the sand before waving toward him. "Okay, you got the GPS. Let's go already."

He nodded but then hesitated. "Our bags."

Her eyes widened. "Who cares about the bags?" she cried desperately. "Forget the bags!"

"Without any supplies, we won't last long," he reasoned. Taking a deep breath, he cautiously shifted his weight so he could reach into the small backseat. His fingers wrapped around the strap of her backpack, and he slowly lifted it out of the backseat. "You better have grabbed some pretty amazing stuff."

Lilly caught the bag when he tossed it up to her. "Bottled water, some energy bars."

"Yummy," he said, voice strained with stress and effort as he reached back down for his own duffel bag. "What else?"

"I did grab..." She trailed off thoughtfully. "Are you just asking me this to distract yourself from the extremely dangerous predicament you're in?"

He rolled his eyes at her comment. "I *was*. But you talking about it kind of defeats the purpose." He tossed the second bag up to her, hitting her in the face with it.

She laughed and tossed it to the side. "Sorry!" Leaning down so she could see the top of his blond head, she called down. "Would it be distracting if I told you I packed skimpy red lingerie and a pair of stiletto pumps?" It was a lie, but it would distract almost any twenty-something male.

Christian gave a surprised bark of laughter at her comment. "Yeah, that's distracting all right." With a shake of his head, he began climbing up along the driver seat. His elbow bumped the horn, and the sound reverberated across the desert.

Despite the gravity of the situation, Lilly snorted with barely suppressed laughter. "Could you make a little less noise with your scrambling? You're waking the neighbors."

He glanced up at her as he got his foot securely at the top of the driver side headrest. "Yeah, because—" What he'd been about to say died in his throat with a grunt of discomfort as the truck slipped a few feet.

"Tex!" she screamed in fear, all humor evaporating in that instant.

The truck groaned again, creaking in protest as it fought to keep from plummeting to the bottom of the chasm.

"Shit," Christian cursed, his eyes wide with distress. Doubling his efforts, he began to frantically climb his way up to the driver's window. He pushed his way through the opening with record speed and sprung to his feet on the side of the car.

Once there, he braced himself. The truck had slipped far enough down that he was going to have to jump to get back up to where Lilly was waiting above. With a deep, steadying breath, he lunged. He hit the ground at his waist. His upper body was safely on sand while his feet dangled into the chasm.

Lilly was at his side in an instant. She grabbed his shirt tightly between her fists and pulled. She could feel her heart pounding wildly in her chest as she struggled to keep her only companion from falling to his death. Slowly, she helped pull him to safety.

With one last grunt of effort, Christian made his way back onto solid ground.

They both collapsed onto their backs in the sand, staring up into the twilight sky.

"You're insane," Lilly said breathlessly.

"Nah. Just practical."

They lay in silence for a few minutes, both trying to catch their breath and let their heartbeats return to normal.

Finally, Lilly turned her head to look at him. "Why did you lie to me?" she asked quietly. She wasn't sure she really wanted to know the answer. After everything they'd been through together, she didn't want to have a reason not to trust him.

He closed his eyes and stayed silent. Lilly thought he was just going to ignore her question, but then he turned his face toward hers and said, "I was afraid if I admitted I knew you before we talked at the pyramids, you would think I was a crazy stalker or something."

"Aren't you?" she asked, raising an eyebrow at him.

"No." He snorted in annoyance. "The truth is..." He rolled

his eyes. "All right, I'll admit I had a bit of a crush on you. When I saw you standing in front of that pyramid, I thought it was a sign."

"So you didn't follow me here?" she asked hopefully.

"No! Of course I didn't. I was here because I wanted to be here. I enjoy traveling. I've been planning this trip for over two years."

"Oh."

"The minute I realized the world might actually be ending, I knew it was more than just a sign. It was fate."

"It's fate that we're meant to be together?" she asked with raised brows. It was hard to keep the skepticism from her voice. His comment made her feel more than a little freaked out. It was on the verge of creepy. She didn't want to commit herself to a man because of a coincidence.

"I think its fate that I was meant to be here when you were. I was meant to get you safely to the pyramids." He hesitated a moment before adding, "Even if it meant dying myself."

She sucked in a gasp of disbelief. "So that's why you risked yourself to throw those supplies up to me?" On his sheepish nod, she rolled onto her stomach, moving closer to him. She placed her palms against his cheeks and gave him a stern glare. "You are more important to me than a few bottles of water."

She stared down at him with half of her upper body draped across his chest. Her heart suddenly picked up speed. He was the most amazing, selfless man she'd ever met. Unable to help herself, not that she wanted to, she lowered her mouth slowly toward his.

Just as their lips were about to meet, a ball of fire roughly the size of a basketball crashed from the sky and slammed into the sand a few yards away from them.

"What the hell was that?" Lilly squeaked.

Christian leaned up to a sitting position, his blue eyes wide.

As he moved, Lilly was forced to sit up as well. Their legs intertwined, and she found herself straddling one of his thighs, though the moment was no longer romantic.

"The ozone is deteriorating," he breathed in horror. "I've read..." He shook his head in disbelief. "Solar flares or something..." He made a noise of frustration. "I wish I had paid more attention. Electronics will be fried, and basically big fire balls are going to burn everything up. In a nutshell, we don't want to be out here in the open and get hit by one of those things."

As if to prove his point, a second fire ball crashed to the earth nearby. The ground trembled with the force of the impact. This caused the truck to finally give way, falling down into the newly created ravine.

"How about we get to that pyramid already?" Lilly requested with anxiety lacing her voice.

Christian nodded emphatically at that suggestion and lunged to his feet, pulling her with him. "If we get there in one piece with this crappy GPS system while dodging solar flares it will be a miracle." He slung his duffel bag over his head. Sweeping her pack up off the desert floor, he shoved it into her hands. "Let's go!"

Lilly quickly slid the backpack on and stared up at him with a new appreciation. "I hope the pyramids are as safe as you promised."

He held a hand out to her, his expression hopeful. "There's only one way to find out."

With a deep breath for courage, she reached out and took his hand. Together, they both turned and raced through the desert, praying their one hope of survival still stood strong.

CHAPTER 7

Lancaster, Pennsylvania
December 22nd, 2012
Erika Kimura

The cabins finally came into view. They were still intact, which was more than anyone could hope for. Erika ignored the burning in her lungs and forced her body to keep moving. The sealed storm cellars that lay innocently next to each cabin were like welcoming beacons.

Max was right on her heels as she ran. She could hear his footfalls hitting the ground just behind her. It was a comforting sound even though she barely knew him. At least she wasn't alone.

As she raced into the camping ground, her eyes swept the door numbers on the outside of the cabins. "Twenty-three, twenty-four, twenty-five, twenty-six, twenty-seven..." The next little cottage made her cry out. "Twenty-eight!"

Max sprinted past her up onto the wooden porch and waved toward the front door. "Unlock it," he hollered over the roaring wind. "Unlock it!"

Erika shook her head as she bypassed the porch and moved to the side of the structure instead. "No! We're not going in the cabin. They'll never stand up against the tornadoes."

Max shot her a look of incredulity. "Then why did we come here?"

She dropped her bag to the ground and bent down in front of the storm cellar. With her heart in her throat, she pulled a chain from around her neck and stared at the cabin key that dangled from it. "For this," she said, holding the chain up for him to see. Turning her attention to the cellar, she took a deep breath, praying the key that opened the cabin door would also open the storm cellar as promised. "This had better work."

Ignoring the harsh pounding of the wind at her back, she took her time lining up the key, hoping it would work. It was the entire reason she'd chosen this place. If it failed, they were more than likely dead.

There was a tense moment of silence as she worked with the lock. Then it sprang free. With a cry of triumph, she removed the lock and tossed it aside. "We're in!"

Max took the large, heavy door from her and held it open while she descended into the darkness below.

"I never thought I'd say this about a musty cellar, but this is perfect. We *will* survive," she said with determination as she dropped her bag to the floor.

Max shot her a crooked grin. "If you would have told me a few days ago that I would happily be spending the night in a dark cellar with an unfamiliar woman, I would have said you were crazy."

Erika responded with an apologetic look. "Speaking of sleeping arrangements... I had an inflatable mattress in the van." She shrugged and motioned to the bags at their feet. "Obviously it was one of the things that got left behind. I'm sorry."

"Sorry?" Max asked with disbelief. "The world as we know it is coming to an end. Millions of people are dead. You just saved me from certain death, and you're sorry because you lost your inflatable air mattress during the rescue?" He waved her off. "Once the storm dies down, I'll head up to the cabins and see if I can salvage a couple good mattresses from the wreckage. Who knows, maybe a few of the cabins might survive intact as well so we can ditch the dank cellar. Either way, you have nothing to be sorry about. Sleeping on a cement floor is the least of my worries right now. At least I'll be alive."

Erika shoved her hands into the back pockets of her jeans, feeling sheepish at his praise. "Yeah..." She trailed off when her fingers brushed her cellular phone. She hadn't checked it since shortly after arriving in the states. With a thoughtful murmur, she pulled it out and glanced at the view screen. One missed call from a few hours ago.

Her eyes widened and she flipped the phone open when she realized she also had a voicemail. "Excuse me," she requested of Max, holding a finger in the air.

He nodded in understanding and moved away to check the security of the storm door while the tornados tore through the land above, offering her some privacy.

Erika dialed into her voicemail while her heart hammered

in her throat. A moment later, she gasped when Tye's voice came over the line.

"Erika," he said softly. "It's me. It's Tye." He let out a soft sigh before continuing. "I wish I was with you right now, sweetheart. I really do." He fell silent, his breathing the only sound on the line. Finally, he spoke again in a gentle tone. "I want you to know that I left Japan. When I saw your flight take off, I knew I had to follow you, whether this turned out to be real or not. I went straight to the ticket counter and got the first flight to the states I could find. The closest they could get me to Lancaster on such short notice was this little town in northern Wyoming." He took a breath then let out a sound of frustration. "I believed you, babe. I really did, but I didn't take the threat seriously enough. I tried calling when I first landed, but the phone lines were busy. I thought it would be a good idea to get a hotel room and sleep off my jetlag before hitting the highway and trying to get through to you again. I'd made it to the states safely after all."

Erika held her breath as she waited for him to continue.

"There's some big volcano in the area," he said. "It chose now of all times to erupt and take out a fourth of the country." He growled unhappily. "When was the last time you heard of a cataclysmic volcano eruption in the states?" He sighed, sounding tired. "I guess this was the kind of thing you were trying to warn me about."

Erika felt dread welling up inside of her. She slid to the floor, fearing what she knew was coming next.

"I'm not going to be able to meet up with you," he admitted softly. "I'm guessing you already figured that out. You're a smart girl." Tears were already streaming down her face when he said, "I'm in the blast zone, sweetheart. In a couple minutes, there isn't going to be anything left. I'm sorry."

Wracking sobs began shaking her shoulders as tears cascaded through the dirt that lined her cheeks. While fighting for her life, she'd been able to put Tye out of her thoughts, but there was no way to ignore his fate anymore. Her fiancé, the person she loved most in the world, was dead.

At that moment, Max came back down the stairs. His eyes widened upon seeing her slumped on the floor. He hurried to her side and crouched in front of her, expression full of concern. Yet he stayed silent upon seeing the desperate way she gripped the phone to her ear. He merely put a comforting hand on her knee as she listened to Tye's final moments.

"I had to call and tell you not to worry about me," Tye continued. "I'm going to be okay. Just knowing you're safe is enough. I'm going to die, but at least I can die happy because *you* are safe. I know it. I can feel it." He made a soft sound of surprise that Erika knew came from something on his end of the line. "I can see the lava from my window. It's...it's amazing. It truly is." There was a moment of silence, and then his voice came through again. "I'm going to go now," he said quietly. "I don't want to miss this show. I just wanted to let you know that I love you. I'll miss you, but hopefully that means you'll live a long life. I'll be waiting on the other side for you." With that, the voicemail abruptly ended.

Erika gave a cry of protest. "No. Not yet! Don't go!" Her entire body gave a shudder of grief. The knowledge that this message was hours old and that Tye had been dead just as long had her quivering with regret. She'd missed his call, his final good-bye. "Don't leave me, Tye! Please, please," she sobbed.

"Erika?" Max asked softly.

"That...that was my fiancé," she managed to explain through her tears. She didn't need to say any more. Max understood. He'd lost his wife a few short hours ago. His pain was nearly as fresh as hers.

Sliding closer on the floor, he pulled her into a hug. "We're going to be okay," he promised. "We'll get through this. Together."

And they did.

12

Burlington, Vermont
Derek Allison

Derek stumbled through the debris laden streets, his focus solely on getting to his daughter. After his car had taken a nosedive into the creek, he'd fought and clawed his way back to land. He felt as if he'd inhaled enough water to fill an entire swimming pool, but he'd made it.

He staggered through the last few blocks to his house, his fear escalating at the damage taken by nearby homes. Before the wreck, he'd heard the news reports about the tornadoes. He wasn't a fool. Anyone could tell this area had been hit and hit hard. He just prayed that his house still stood, that Peyton and Melody were inside and safe.

In his heart, he could admit to himself that his wife was dead. Nearly everyone in Japan was dead. His only hope was that his daughter hadn't suffered the same fate.

With his pulse pounding against his temple, he turned down the road that would lead to his home. His neighbors' homes were in different states of disrepair. Most were totally destroyed, while some still held some of their foundation.

As he staggered past an overturned Prius, he realized that there wasn't a person to be found anywhere. His eyes landed on the body of his next door neighbor, Jack, and he had to fight back the bile in his throat as he corrected that there was no one *alive* to be found. There were plenty of bodies strewn along the streets, though. His already dismal spirits fell further.

"Please," he begged. "Please let my daughter be alive, my little Melody." His words broke off with a sob that was drowned out by the still roaring wind. "Melody!" he screamed in agony.

Any hope he had died the instant his eyes landed on his home. There was nothing left but bits of wood and debris. The entire structure had caved in, most of it crumbling into the basement. Anyone inside would have been trapped underneath two levels worth of rubble.

There wasn't a single hope of anyone surviving if they'd been inside while the tornadoes tore through. His entire family had perished. "Why?" he screamed with anguish into the rain. "Why them? You should have taken me! Not my daughter! Why do I get to live?"

His shouts were answered by the storm, almost as if it was informing him that perhaps he wasn't as lucky as he thought and that he wouldn't be permitted to live after all. It felt as if he was only going to be allowed to live long enough to realize he'd lost everything before being struck down.

The wind picked up in intensity and lightning lit the sky. The wind beat relentlessly at one of the few trees left standing, ripping its roots from the ground and tossing it carelessly to the side.

Realizing that his life was indeed in danger, Derek stumbled backwards into the road, his eyes wide. His mind grasped desperately for a safe shelter, somewhere he could hole up until he could decide a new plan of action. Even if there was very little hope, he wouldn't give up searching for his daughter. He would dig tirelessly through the rubble of his home until there was proof that his daughter had been killed.

The tornado shelter a few houses down entered his mind. If anything had survived, it was that. Struggling against the bruising winds, he made his way slowly but surely toward the shelter.

As he moved, his thoughts went to his last conversation with Peyton. He'd all but demanded she stay put until he got home. It was his fault they'd been inside the house when the tornado ripped it apart. He should have told her to get to safety, not stay put and wait for him.

His soul was full of regret as he reached the shelter. The doors were tightly shut, but he managed to pry them open. Feeling like a coward, feeling defeated, he slunk into the shelter. He closed the doors behind him and descended into the dark cellar that felt more like a tomb to him than protection.

It was only when he got to the bottom of the steps that he saw the soft glow coming from a battery powered lantern. "Hello?" he called out nervously. He was breaking and entering, but surely his neighbors would understand in a time like this.

"Daddy?" a little girl's voice cried from behind the light.

Derek squinted, unable to see who stood behind the glow. "Melody?" he whispered, terrified to even hope.

"Daddy!" His daughter's unmistakable voice echoed off

the walls as she squealed with delight. Then she was throwing herself into his arms. "I knew you'd find us."

"Oh, Melody," he breathed, stooping down so he could envelope the child in his arms. "My sweet, sweet girl." Tears were streaming down his cheeks as he clutched her to his chest in disbelief.

The lamp shifted and suddenly Peyton was staring down at him. Her blue eyes were full of worry. "I know you said not to leave the house, but things got really scary. I disobeyed your orders, and I realize that isn't acceptable. I'm sorry if I worried you."

Standing, Derek lifted Melody to his hip and put a comforting hand on Peyton's shoulder. "You did great. Sometimes orders need to be ignored. Had you listened to me…" He trailed off, not even wanting to think about that frightening alternative. He didn't want to scare them any further, but he also felt the need to be honest. "Everything up there is gone."

Peyton looked like she'd been about to say something, but his last comment stopped her in her tracks. "Everything? What do you mean everything is gone?"

"Everything," he affirmed. "My house, the neighbor's house, the entire neighborhood. I haven't seen a single living soul since before…" He didn't want to admit in front of his daughter that he'd crashed his car and had to drag himself up the banks of Otter Creek. "It's been a while," he finally concluded, leaving out any details that might frighten a four-year-old any further.

Peyton sunk to the ground with a stunned expression. "How? I don't believe it."

"The tornadoes," Derek explained. "They destroyed everything."

"But we're safe, Daddy," Melody assured. "Jamie said we would be."

"Jamie?" he asked in confusion.

Peyton blushed and ducked her head in embarrassment. "My boyfriend." Her head shot up as she quickly assured, "He never comes over when I babysit Melody. I promise. He was just worried. He thought we should go somewhere safer."

"Smart boy," Derek said before glancing around for the teenager who had most likely saved his little girl's life. "Where is Jamie? I should thank him personally for getting the two of you out of there. Had you listened to me, you would have been dead."

He ceased looking for the boy the instant he saw the tears welling in Peyton's eyes. They made a trail down her dirt-stained cheeks as she turned her face away to wipe at them.

Melody tugged on his suit jacket, and he lowered his gaze to her. "He's with Jesus now, Daddy. He's probably bowling in heaven right now."

Derek's gaze swept swiftly back to Peyton.

She laughed softly at Melody's comment as she swiped once again at her tears. "He's definitely bowling right now." A faint smile touched her lips. "He always did look really cute in bowling shoes." Her comment brought a choked sob from her throat.

Derek stooped down in front of Peyton and pulled her gently into a hug. They were so different from one another. They were different sexes, from different ethnic back-grounds, and were from different generations, but they'd both lost someone they loved.

After what she'd sacrificed for his child, Peyton was fam-ily. She was like a second daughter to him now. He smiled faintly when she relaxed into him, resting her head tiredly against his shoulder as she cried.

While they took shelter from the storm, Derek hugged his two girls and whispered words of comfort in their ears. He knew in his heart they would make it through this. They would be safe and live to tell future generations of the hor-rors they'd witnessed this day.

12

Denver, Colorado
Jacob Williams

Jacob sat on the hotel bed, his elbows on his knees with his hands clasped together in front of him. His eyes were trained on Molly as she sat in the window overlooking the burning wreckage of the plane crash.

Her shoulders were hunched, and he could see her arms trembling where they hugged her knees to her chest. He knew he should say some words of comfort to her, but he didn't have anything left in him to offer. All of the occupants that had been at the hotel only a few hours before were dead. All of the people in the plane who had tried to escape were dead. If he was honest with himself, Ryan was probably dead as well.

As if reading his thoughts, Molly asked, "Are you sure your brother is coming?" Her voice was a defeated whisper, and she didn't even turn from the window to look at him. It was as if she couldn't bear it.

Jacob's stomach flipped anxiously at the mention of his brother. It had been hours with no contact. Perhaps it was silly to even hope at this point, but hope was all he had left. "He'll be here," he finally said in a firm voice. "If...if something had happened to him, I'd know." He shook his head. "No. He's still out there. I know it."

He didn't appreciate the pitying look she sent him when at last she turned from the window. Her eyes were a pretty green filled with compassion, a compassion he didn't like having directed at him. "He'll be here," he repeated stubbornly.

Molly's grim expression fell away as she gave him a soft smile of optimism. "I believe you." She shrugged. "I have faith in your conviction. He's out there somewhere."

A silence fell around them, and Molly turned back to the window. Neither one wanted to say that the longer Ryan was missing, the less likely it was he had survived. Determination and willpower could only get a person so far during an onslaught of natural disasters. Though Jacob knew Ryan would never give up, sometimes a person was overpowered by events out of their control.

As his thoughts once again turned grim, Molly suddenly

bolted upright with a gasp. "Looks like you may be right," she said, eagerly waving him over. "There's a truck!" She whipped to face him with wide eyes. "Someone just pulled up to the front of the building."

Jacob raced to the window and peered down at the familiar vehicle. "That's Ryan's truck!" Pushing off the window frame, he ran to the door and threw it open.

"Wait for me," Molly cried, chasing after him. "I'm coming with you!"

Grabbing her hand, Jacob pulled her after him down the stairs that separated them from the front doors of the hotel. "Ryan!" he called loudly. "Ryan!" He hit the landing, took the corner blindly, and smacked into someone.

There was a feminine grunt as someone bounced off his chest.

Instinctively, he reached out and steadied the woman's shoulders. It took him a few confused moments to focus on her face and realize who it was. "Penny!"

"Jake!" She pulled him into a crushing hug. "Oh, Jake! Thank God you're okay."

Jacob held her against his chest for a few moments, clutching her tightly as if afraid she might vanish if he let go. Finally, he pulled back to look at her. "Penny, where's Ryan?"

It was only now that he really took in her appearance. She had dried tear tracks streaking down the dirt caked on her face. She was filthy and disheveled. It was obvious she'd been through a lot. Her unkempt state had his stomach tightening with worry. He hated to push her, but he had to know. "Where's my brother? What happened?"

Her blue eyes widened and a fresh sob escaped her. "Shortly after we got off the phone with you, a dog ran out in front of Ryan's truck. He had to swerve to miss it and accidentally ran off the road. We got stuck in this ditch and with the mud..." Tearfully, she filled him in on how Ryan had gotten trapped under the boulder. "I tried so hard to get his leg free, but I just wasn't strong enough. He...he begged me to leave him."

Jacob's eyes widened in horror, and he glanced behind Penny, willing his brother to come sauntering around the corner. "And?" he asked hoarsely. "Did you?"

She blinked at him for a moment before swiping at her tears with the back of her hand. "I didn't want to leave him.

12

Just the thought was like tearing a hole through my heart, but he said he couldn't bear for me to watch him drown, and he wanted you to know what happened to him. It was a horrible thing for him to ask of me. I never wanted to leave his side, ever again," she whimpered.

Jacob's shoulders sagged at her anguished expression.

"And she didn't have to," came Ryan's unmistakable voice as he rounded the corner, carrying a little girl on his hip.

"Ryan!" Jacob rushed to his brother and pulled him into a one-armed hug as best as he could without crushing the girl.

Penny continued wiping at her tears, but more were falling down her cheeks. "I refused to leave him. Lucky for us both, a van drove by shortly after he was trapped."

Ryan picked up where she left off. "The van was packed full of kids. Orphans," he added. "They'd been abandoned."

"This amazing couple, Jack and Mary, had rounded the kids up and were trying to get them to safety," Penny interjected. "Jack helped get Ryan out from under the boulder."

Ryan shifted the little girl to his other hip so she could face Jacob. "Melissa here rode in the truck with Penny and me. She was the only child riding without a seatbelt. She'd been on Mary's lap in their van."

Jacob saw the look of affection for the girl in his brother's eyes. It only surprised him for a moment. He supposed his brother could sympathize with an abandoned child left to fend for herself. Offering the girl a nonthreatening smile, he said, "Hello, Melissa. I'm Jacob, Ryan's brother."

The little girl gave him an adorable smile before shyly tucking her face against Ryan's neck. "Hi, Jacob," she mumbled angelically, her voice muffled by Ryan's shirt.

With a lopsided grin, Jacob returned his attention to Ryan. "So where is this van full of orphans? Are they unloading?"

Ryan shot Penny a look before limping forward to hand Melissa to her. "They're not coming."

Jacob had been about to start out the building to help bring everyone inside when Ryan's words stopped him in his tracks. "They're not coming?"

Penny shook her head and dropped to her knees in front of the little girl. She began smoothing out Melissa's tangled hair, fussing over her as she wiped a smudge of dirt off of the girl's cheek as if it would help her scruffy appearance.

Jacob's eyes widened. "But what about..." His gaze shot

pointedly to Melissa before returning to his brother.

"The storms and disasters are dying down," Ryan said, not answering his brother's unfinished question. "It looks like the worst is over." He shook his head with a grim expression. "Last I heard, they estimated ninety-six percent of the population in the United States is gone, ninety-four worldwide."

Jacob had to reach out to the wall for support to keep from collapsing to the floor in shock. "Ninety...ninety-six percent?" he asked in horror.

Ryan nodded. "The next few years are going to be all about rebuilding. Things are going to be crazy for a long time. We could be the only people for fifty miles, Jake."

Jacob ran a hand over his forehead in disbelief. "But there were people here only a few hours ago. Surely all of them weren't killed by the tornadoes." He whipped to Molly, feeling desperate. "Tell him."

She nodded her emphatic agreement. "It's true. The lobby downstairs was filled with people."

Ryan offered them an apologetic shrug. "Most of the buildings in the surrounding areas are gone. The airport is gone. All that's left is this hotel, and not even all of it is standing. You are damn lucky to be alive, Jake."

Jacob's face paled at how close he'd come to losing his life. He'd known things were grim, but he hadn't realized the full weight of the situation until now. He'd been so worried about his brother that he hadn't taken his own safety into consideration. "That's...that's impossible."

Ryan shook his head sadly. "Unfortunately, it *is* possible." He took a deep breath before pressing on. "A few of the orphans were injured. We heard over an emergency broadcast there was a hospital in San Diego that still had emergency power. They're taking in people who need medical attention."

He shot an affectionate grin toward Penny and Melissa, his eyes twinkling. "Melissa didn't need any medical attention, and it wasn't safe how she was riding in the van." His eyes slid back to Jacob. "With this catastrophe, there are probably going to be even more orphans out there. It's going to be tough keeping them clothed and fed."

He took another deep breath and pushed on determinedly. "With all that in mind, we decided to keep Melissa." Making sure his brother knew exactly what he was saying, Ryan added, "I guess you could say I adopted her, Jake. She's mine."

Jacob had come to suspect this outcome the moment Ryan stated the rest of the orphans weren't coming, but hearing it out loud had him rocking back on his feet in surprise. No matter how much he saw it coming, this was big news. "She's yours?" he asked in awe. He turned to really look at the girl.

He would guess her age to be around three. She had long, curly brown hair nearly to her waist. Large, hazel eyes filled up the majority of her face as she peered up at his brother with adoration. Her cheeks were dirty, but she was an adorable little thing.

"They're our family now," Ryan said softly to his brother before limping over to the two girls. He put a hand on Penny's shoulder and leaned down to kiss her tenderly.

When he pulled back, Penny beamed up at him. "I'm going to take Melissa to the bathroom to wash up. Hopefully the showers will still be working."

Ryan's hand trailed along her back as Penny followed Molly toward the stairs that led up to the hotel room. Once they disappeared, he turned back to his brother, a goofy grin stretched across his lips.

"What happened?" Jacob asked in astonishment. "When you left the house this morning, you were a single bachelor. Now you're...you're...a dad? And back with Penny?"

"I always wanted a family, Jake. And I wanted it with Penny. This is my second chance to have all of that. Melissa needs us." His eyes searched his brother's face for understanding.

Without hesitation, Jacob clapped a hand to Ryan's shoulder. "Well, congrats, bro." He shook his head with a laugh. "You are the only man on the face of the planet under thirty to seek out a ready-made family, but I'm happy for you."

Ryan grinned and shook him off. "I wanted to do for Melissa what Gram did for us."

"She's a lucky little girl," Jacob said honestly as Ryan followed him, limping, up to the hotel room. "You know I've got your back on this. I'll help in any way I can."

Ryan reached out to ruffle his younger brother's hair. "I wouldn't have it any other way."

San Fernando Valley, California
Clara Dichello

Clara sat in the bowels of an underground bomb shelter, but it was like none she'd ever heard of. Instead of cement walls and a square block of space, it was like the inside of an apartment. There were two bedrooms, a bathroom, a kitchen, and a large living room. It was attractively furnished and spacious. Down here, it felt as if life hadn't been turned completely upside down. She sat on a stool at the kitchen table and stared at Benjamin from across her hot cup of cappuccino.

When their eyes met, he looked quickly down into his own cup. He'd been playing the shy, silent game ever since they'd sat down across the small table from one another.

Likewise, she had no clue what to say to him. A few hours ago, she'd been accusing him of being a perverted stalker. She couldn't have been farther from the truth. She felt guilty for her treatment of him in the past, but had no clue how to even start to repair things. "This is a nice place you have here," she finally said in an attempt at conversation. "For a bomb shelter."

"Yeah," he replied, running a hand along the back of his neck and rolling his eyes. "Everyone thought I was crazy for building a giant bomb shelter, but they weren't about to turn down my money."

"You were rich then?" she asked. "Before all of this?"

"I was well off, but by no means was I rich," Benjamin informed her. "I put a lot of my wages into making this shelter. I was a lawyer, and I made good money, but it was mostly my connections that gave me any sort of power."

"Is that how you found me?" Clara asked, not sure whether she should feel offended or honored. "Through your connections?"

"Yes," he stated simply. Then he followed his comment with an annoyed snort. "The legal system made that task very difficult. There are so many laws and identity protection blocks for adopted children. I knew I had a sister out there, a twin sister. It just took me forever to find you."

"Because of the pesky laws?" Clara asked, raising an

12

eyebrow.

"I'm getting chastised by a porn star about moral ethics?" he asked with a chuckle.

Clara couldn't help but laugh in return. She supposed he had a point there. "Some family we are. Both of us chose professions in ethically immoral fields."

"There's nothing ethically immoral about being a lawyer."

"Says the man who broke a few laws to track down his porn star sister."

Benjamin grinned, and Clara was surprised to feel her chest swelling with pride. Her brother was a hottie. "I finally get why you never hit on me," she said with a sound of relief. "I always thought you were a weirdo trying to 'save' me from my ungodly life. Here you were just trying to get to know me."

He shrugged. "That was all that really mattered. I wanted to make sure you were happy with your life. I'll admit I was a tad shocked when I discovered how you earned a paycheck. I had a hard time trying to figure out what to say to you."

"You didn't know what to say so instead you stalked me!" she accused with a laugh. "I was freaked out!"

"I'm sorry," Benjamin apologized, his hazel eyes full of sincerity. "I just didn't know what to say. I didn't even know where to begin. You're a grown woman. I couldn't be sure you'd want me in your life even after you knew who I was, and I'd broken a few laws to track you down. If anyone found out..." He frowned and waved toward her elaborate dress. "And you're quite the intimidating woman. You make men nervous, even those not trying to hit on you."

Reaching out, Clara covered his hand with hers. "Well, I'm glad you didn't give up. You saved my life tonight. I would definitely love for you to be in it."

"Got choice?" he asked derisively.

It was true that they didn't have much choice but to be around one another, but she wasn't as grim about it as he might think. "On the bright side, we'll definitely get to know each other down here," she said, trying to sound positive.

Benjamin's lips curled into a pleased grin. "I'd really like that."

"Me too," Clara whispered, and was surprised that she truly meant it. She was a very private person, but sitting across from her was the confidant she'd been missing her entire life. He was real flesh and blood, a brother.

The first sob escaped her before she realized it was coming. The one that followed, she was incapable of halting. Soon, she was crying full out as the events of the past twenty-four hours caught up with her. She had lost Bruce, but that cruel forfeiture of life had brought her the bittersweet joy of finding her brother.

Benjamin hesitated only a moment before making his way around the table to pull her into a timid hug.

"I'm so glad you found me," she sobbed into his shoulder, clinging tightly to him to let Benjamin know there was no shame in holding her. They were family. With tears streaming down her cheeks, she clung to the man who had suddenly become the most important person in her life. She had a brother, and he would take care of her.

Lilly Singh
The Pyramid of Khufu at Giza
Just Outside of Cairo, Egypt
December 22nd, Morning

Though she was exhausted and barely able to stay up-right, Lilly let out a whoop of joy as the Khufu pyramid loomed even closer ahead of them. Now that they were nearly to the pyramid, she could see that it had sustained some damage, but was in relatively good shape. It would be a great place for them to take shelter for a while. "We made it! Unbelievable! We made it!" She spun to Christian, her eyes wide with excitement. "All your navigation crap worked!"

He smiled in response, blue eyes sparkling with just as much joy as hers. "I told you it would work!" Picking her up in his arms, he spun her around with a hearty laugh before depositing her back on her feet in the sand.

Lilly stared up at him and licked her dry lips. He was definitely looking pretty ragged. Sand stuck in the beads of sweat clinging to his forehead. His shirt was torn across his left bicep, blood staining the ripped fabric from a cut he'd gotten during the truck fiasco. The knee of his jeans where he'd shattered the passenger window was also in shreds, blood caking the thick material. He was a total mess, but she'd never seen a more attractive man in her life. "Are you going to kiss me already or what?" she asked after their eyes had lingered on each other's for far too long.

"I thought you didn't date Christians?" he asked with surprise.

Though his statement was cautious, she noted that his hands stayed firmly on her waist, his fingers sliding softly along her shirt. "I've been thinking about making an exception to that rule," she informed him with a crooked grin.

His smile matched hers as he pulled her toward him and lowered his head to capture her mouth with his. His kiss was timid and searching, his lips caressing tentatively along hers.

Lilly let his gentle kiss go on a moment before throwing her arms around his neck and deepening it. He didn't need to be shy or hold back with her. They'd been through too much together for that.

The next few minutes were spent this way, with her arms thrown around his neck and both of them clinging to the other while their kiss continued on. She felt almost like a Disney princess, suspended in this one magical moment with a hero beyond human standards.

"Hello?" a voice called out, breaking into their enchanted escape from reality. "Is someone out there?"

The couple jumped apart and stared at each other with wide eyes.

Christian turned toward the pyramid where the sound had come from and hollered back. "Yes! We're here!" Taking Lilly's hand, he led her toward the figure that had bolted out of the pyramid at the sound of his voice and was running toward them.

Lilly hesitated upon seeing a gun strapped across the person's shoulder. The figure was feminine, but a gun usually didn't mean anything good, especially one that large.

"It's okay," Christian encouraged. "She's military. American," he added in surprise as the woman got closer.

Lilly squinted at the woman, wanting to confirm this for herself.

The stranger had shoulder length red hair pulled back in a tight ponytail that did nothing to control the frizz brought on by desert heat. Freckles spotted her tan face and large green eyes dominated her features. She was wearing a United States Army uniform that had seen better days. "Where did you come from?" she asked in breathless disbelief as she reached them. On their confused looks, she continued, "Jerry and I have been searching for survivors all day. Cairo is completely gone. There's nothing left." She shook her head, eyes wide with astonishment. "Our whole platoon was there when things went down. Jerry and I were separated from the rest because we were out on an assignment. When we got back, the base was totally destroyed with no sign of anyone. Despite the fact that it looked like no one survived, we've been trying to get in touch with any of them on their radios all morning without any luck. We'd hoped that some of our people got out, but the radio channel has been silent since yesterday. I fear there isn't much hope...anywhere. You two are lucky to be alive, very lucky."

With that, the woman nodded toward the pyramid. "Fol-

12

low me." She started toward the structure with a sigh. "Like I said, we have been searching for survivors all morning. We'd all but given up hope, especially after Jerry hurt his leg. We were forced to stop looking so he could recover. We thought there was no one left to save anyway."

She shook her head vigorously in disbelief. "We gave up hope on finding others, and then you two stumbled upon *us*." She tossed them a friendly smile. "I'm Rebecca, by the way."

"I'm Lilly." Lilly quickly rushed out the next bit before Christian could introduce himself. "This is my boyfriend Christian."

"Well, welcome Lilly and Christian. Welcome to the safest place in the world right now." She motioned toward a military vehicle parked outside the pyramid entrance that looked completely out of place. "We were lucky enough that our vehicle survived. We filled it with enough supplies to last us a few months while we were at what was left of the base. Supplies were the only things we managed to find." She shook her head sadly and crossed her fingers over her heart in respect for her lost comrades. "Jerry plans to start working on one of our damaged helicopters at the base as soon as his leg is a little better. It may take a while to get it running, but we should be able to get back to what's left of the states."

As Rebecca raced into the pyramid, Lilly tried to keep her head from spinning. *What was left?*

"Hey," Christian said, interrupting her worries. "What was with the boyfriend comment?" He elbowed her playfully. "Are you getting overprotective already?"

Lilly shot him a look of annoyance, yet she couldn't help but laugh at his comically smug expression. "I'm just trying to make sure you don't change your mind and pursue a bubbly redhead."

He snorted in response. "Please! I did not fight this hard to get you to notice me only to blow it. You're stuck with me, I'm afraid."

Lilly rolled her eyes, but she was smiling. "I suppose there's no one else I'd rather be stuck with."

"You suppose?" he cried spiritedly. "Don't make me go back there and toss you down with the truck!"

It was her turn to elbow him. "As if you could! You've had the hots for me for way too long to do something as foolish as that."

Christian grabbed her waist and pulled her in against his side. "That's right I did." He started walking, guiding her toward the pyramid entrance. "Now, let's get in there so I can go all caveman on Jerry about your committed status. I'd like to get that over with so we can move on to helping preserve the future and rebuilding our lives."

Lilly stared up at him with admiration because she knew he truly meant that. He would work hard to help make a better world for the people left in it. Together, *they* would make a better world.

12

The Forbidden City
Beijing, China
March 28th, 2013

Nikki lay in a small room that had been transformed into a bedroom in the Forbidden City. The building was no longer a museum. It was now being used for its original purpose as a home, though no emperors lived here, only refugees from the apocalypse. Most were China natives, but there was a plethora of nations mingled in the old structures.

Nikki lay in her bed, curled up in blankets as she fought to keep warm. Three months had passed since the disasters that nearly destroyed earth. Survivors were trying to piece things back together, but the future was still full of uncertainty.

With a depressed sigh, she grabbed the remote on her bedside table and hit play to view the content on the DVD in the player. She was honored that she'd been allowed to have it and the television in front of her, two of the few electronics that had survived the solar flares. More were being fixed every day, but as a semi-celebrity from her dismal last news assignment, she was permitted to have some of the first un-covered.

Last month, someone had discovered a working com-puter and had been able to transfer the data on Scott's memory card, which he'd slipped into her jacket pocket at some point during their last few hours together, to DVD. Now she was able to watch those last miserable days as often as she wished. It was torture to watch her friends die over and over again, but it was the last connection she had to home. The last connection she had to Scott.

Dejectedly, she watched as Tony and Pearson fumbled their way through the hotel lobby in Nagoya. Back then, they hadn't known that three of them would be dead within a few hours.

Shivering, she moved the footage back a few chapters to the filmed sexual encounter between herself and Scott. She'd seen this video enough times to have it memorized.

She didn't watch it because it brought her any arousal, but because it was one of the very few clips that included

Scott. He'd always been behind the camera, forever an ob-
server lost to time. She lovingly studied his familiar features
on this rare clip as he made love to her. That's what it had
been, love. He'd loved her, but she'd been too blind to see it
until it was too late. He'd loved her so much that he'd given
his own life for hers.

There was a knock at the door, so Nikki quickly paused
the video, making sure the frozen frame was decent enough
with neither her nor Scott exposed. "Come in."

Xiu, the girl from the helicopter, peeked her head into the
room. "I have lunch."

Nikki waved a hand, motioning for her to come into the
room. "Thank you." She sat up in bed with a groan. "I could
have come to the kitchen. You didn't have to bring this to me."

To be honest, Xiu had been taking care of her a lot during
these last three months. On most days, Nikki found it too
hard to even get out of bed. She knew there were others
who had lost loved ones, but she couldn't function around
the pain. She was alone here in a foreign country. She'd lost
everyone and everything. She didn't even have her home-
land to cling to for hope. Without Xiu, she would have with-
ered away to nothing by now.

"Thank you, Xiu," she repeated softly, pulling the tray,
which held a bowl of rice and a small plate of vegetables, toward her.

"Do not worry over it," the girl assured. "You need your
rest." She pulled a bottle of water from her pocket and set it
down on the tray. As she did, her eyes flicked to the television then back to Nikki. "He must have loved you very
much." She covered Nikki's hand with one of hers. "He would
be happy to know the two of you are safe."

"I know he—" Nikki broke off with a look of surprise. She
blinked at Xiu in confusion. "The two of us?"

"Well, yes," Xiu responded, looking just as confused.
"You and the baby."

Nikki continued to blink. Over the past three months,
she'd gotten used to Xiu's accent. The lilt and cadence of
Xiu's voice was now a comfort to her. The language barrier
they'd faced in the beginning was all but nonexistent now,
but she was not following the girl. After a full minute of silence, she asked, "The baby?"

Xiu's eyes lowered to Nikki's abdomen. "Yes..."

12

Nikki's entire world shifted in that moment. "I'm pregnant?" she breathed, her voice barely above a whisper.

Xiu's dark eyes swept to Nikki's face. They were wide with astonishment. "You did not know?"

"No." Nikki's mind raced through the past few months. She'd been so caught up in mourning for Scott that she'd neglected to pay attention to anything else. Now she saw the signs. Her menstrual cycle had been nonexistent since two weeks before that horrendous day. She'd been getting nauseous every morning for the last two months. Recently, even though she hadn't been eating much, she'd begun to gain weight. She could tell by the fit of her clothing. She'd never given any of this any thought, until now. "I had no clue," she confided.

"This is good news, yes?" the dark-haired girl inquired. "Your baby will be one to rebuild," she said in stilted English. "A baby of the future. She is the next generation."

Nikki tentatively placed a hand over her belly. "It is good news. It's just...shocking." It was nearly impossible to believe that under her palm rested her child, Scott's child. "I didn't lose him," she said on a sob. "Not completely." She pictured a little boy with Scott's eyes, his smile. That would be *her* little boy, her reason for living.

The past three months had been spent mourning the dead, but this afternoon, her priorities had shifted. She wouldn't stay depressed and reclusive another moment. She would now cling to life instead of despair.

Scott might be gone, but she would always have a part of him with her. Their child was a symbol of hope when she had none. "My baby is the future." With newfound joy, she realized she was eager to face the upcoming path that lay ahead of her. She was prepared to face the unknown future head on, because she would not be doing so alone. "I love you, Scott," she directed toward the television. Her eyes lifted heavenward. "Thank you for this gift, for a new beginning."

ABOUT THE AUTHOR

Melissa Hosack lives near Pittsburgh, Pennsylvania with her husband Jeremy, their son Marshall Frost, and their four pets Duke, Edge, Eddie, and Leia. She is currently attending London's School of Journalism in their creative writing program.

She runs and edits a government newsletter for Western Pennsylvania titled 'The Patriot' in which she writes a monthly short story column. She has had two novels published by Whimsical Publications as well as multiple short stories through Evernight Publishing.